TEA IS FOR TEMPTATION

A HAUNTED TEAROOM COZY MYSTERY

KAREN SUE WALKER

ACKNOWLEDGEMENTS

All the Tearoom covers are by Mariah Sinclair, the Cozy Cover Queen. You can find her at https://www.thecovervault.com or on Facebook.

Thank you to Alyssa Lynn Palmer for your copyediting expertise.

Special thanks to my beta readers, typo catchers, early reviewers, and all my readers—I'm so grateful to you for your support!

Sign up for email updates at https://karensuewalker.com and I'll do my best to keep your inbox full of everything cozy.

CHAPTER 1

A heavy silence filled the kitchen of my Victorian home and tearoom. The electric clock on the wall ticked away the minutes.

The mound of flour in the bowl looked wrong. Did I measure three cups or four?

"April May, what's gotten into you?" I asked myself, though I knew the answer.

I took a second mixing bowl out of the cabinet and measured again, willing myself to pay attention this time. I'd prepared scones often enough I should be able to make them in my sleep.

The first time the ghost of Chef Emile Toussaint had watched me make scones, he called my prizewinning recipe "peasant food." Later, he told me he was always in the kitchen watching and listening, except now he wasn't—and never would be again.

Swallowing against the lump in my throat, I concentrated on putting three level cups of flour in the bowl. You can't be mad at a dead person for finally getting to heaven after decades of haunting a kitchen, right?

Chef Emile had asked God to reunite him with Marie, the love of his life from his days as a culinary student in Paris. Decades after his death, his prayers had been answered. I smiled at the image of Chef as a young man from Louisiana perfecting his French accent to pass in the elite culinary world he aspired to join. I was happy that he'd found his version of heaven, but selfishly sad for me.

At the sound of Jennifer's footsteps on the stairs, I hurriedly wiped my brimming eyes, but my young, live-in assistant and friend caught me, anyway.

"Oh, April," she said, coming over and wrapping an arm around my waist. "He wouldn't want you to be sad."

Unlike some people in my life, Jennifer completely accepted my ability to see spirits from the moment I shared the information with her. She was already special to me, but that acceptance only made her dearer to my heart.

Given the difference in our ages, I should have been mothering her, but Jennifer had been a warm source of comfort since Chef moved on to the next phase of his afterlife. She clucked over me like a proper mother hen and for the most part, I let her.

"I know he wouldn't," I said in a hoarse voice, "but I miss him so much. Cooking isn't the same without Chef telling me everything I'm doing wrong."

Giving me a little squeeze, she said, "I loved to listen

to you two bickering even if I couldn't hear his side of the conversation."

My laugh came out more like a sob. "That talking-to-myself excuse was pretty unconvincing, huh?"

She chuckled. "Look on the bright side. Chef has his happily ever after, and maybe it's time for you to think about your own future. Your life has bloomed in Serenity Cove, like the flowers in the new secret garden are budding. Those are joyful things, right?"

I couldn't help but feel a little better in the face of her boundless enthusiasm. "You're too young to be so wise."

She gave me a radiant, slightly mischievous smile. "Does that mean you'll listen to me and call Sheriff Fontana?"

Anderson Fontana and I had a complicated relationship. First, I had implicated his wife—soon to be ex-wife—in a murder. Then, the rumors about our non-existent affair had played a major role in an attempt to get him recalled from office.

Jennifer's question was my signal to change the subject—sort of. "I need to finish these scones," I said, reaching for the baking powder, "and his divorce isn't final yet. Do we have any reservations today?"

My half-answer wouldn't have fooled any of my friends. There was no secret that I found the sheriff attractive, but rebound relationships were a bad idea.

To my relief, Jennifer seemed willing to let the matter of my love life go, moving instead to our complicated espresso machine. My mouth watered at the thought of one of her delicious, frothy creations.

She shattered my illusion that she'd moved on from the subject of my love life. "I think you and the sheriff would make a cute couple."

The look on my face must have told her I really couldn't face that topic first thing in the morning with no caffeine. To say the men I'd met since I came to Serenity Cove hadn't worked out for me would be an understatement.

Shortly after moving to town, I'd dated a charming stranger I'd met on my fiftieth birthday. He'd ended up chasing me around the attic with a knife.

Then there was my handsome handyman, Mark. Just as we began to get close, the whole talking-to-ghosts thing drove him out of town. He was also arrested for murder, but that was another story.

My better instincts told me to stay away from Sheriff Fontana, at least for the time being. But I admit, the temptation was nearly strong enough for me to throw caution to the wind.

Jennifer twisted the dials on the coffee machine. "I'll start on the sandwiches when I'm done here. We have four reservations for afternoon tea, and the lunch crowd will be crazy again. Are you getting tired of all the locals who keep asking you to open for dinner?"

"They can ask, but the answer's still going to be no." I'd never wanted to run a full-service restaurant, and the tearoom kept me busy enough. "Besides, what they really want is the Mermaid Café. I'd never live up to their expectations."

The café and its proprietress, my friend Irma Vargas, were local institutions. Losing the building during a devastating storm was a real blow to the community.

With only three other dining options in town, TacoTaco, Tony's Pizza, and the overpriced hotel dining room, the regulars were begging Irma to rebuild and swamping my tearoom in the meantime.

So far Irma refused to even consider the idea of rebuilding, in part because she secretly enjoyed all the rave, nostalgic reviews of her food and the café's funky, underwater vibe. But I knew she felt heartsick over the loss of her beautiful and quirky restaurant.

Since it was June and the tourist business had slowly picked up with the improving weather, I'd gone back to a six-day week for the tearoom to take up some of the slack. We were closed on Mondays, but the lunch crowds for the rest of the week strained us to capacity.

Irma confided to me she might go to work at the hotel. In Irma's mind, she could walk right up, get the job, and immediately help the kitchen staff upgrade the menu. I secretly worried that her plan wouldn't pan out well. Irma wasn't known for her diplomacy. Quite the opposite, in fact.

Our crusty friend's Plan B involved me turning my tearoom into a new, smaller version of the Mermaid Café by night. Even in the face of her wheedling, I said no.

There wasn't enough room in the kitchen for both of us, and I worried Irma would expect me to don something like her trademark mermaid costume and wig. I didn't have the hips to pull off a tail fin. More importantly, I didn't want to create a situation that would put our friendship at risk.

With so much spare time on her hands, Irma was already driving her recently discovered granddaughter, Zoe, half mad with her wild travel ideas, outdated fashion tips, and pointed suggestions that Zoe needed to sign up for college and make something of herself.

A few days earlier, Zoe had stormed through the back door on her way to see Whisk, the Bengal cat who lived in my attic. The two adored one another, and since I'd asked Whisk for advice more than once, I understood Zoe's desire to be alone with him.

As she went by, I asked, "Do you want to talk about it?"

Zoe stopped with her foot on the bottom stair and declared, "I'm something *already!*" before stomping out of sight.

So, we were all dealing with changes—and some of us weren't doing so well.

That Wednesday, the lunch rush and the four reservations for afternoon tea saved me. Between cooking and cleaning, I managed not to think about Chef. By the time the last dish was done, and Jennifer and Zoe were upstairs immersed in yet another viewing of *Pride and Prejudice*, all I wanted to do was relax by the fire with a cup of my favorite rose petal black tea. I brewed a fresh pot and carried my teacup and a plate of cookies to the sofa and propped my feet on the ottoman.

I nearly jumped out of my chair when a polite

cough sounded behind me. Had I forgotten to lock the door again? Or could it be...?

Whirling around with my heart in my throat, I saw a ghost all right, but it wasn't Chef.

The spirit of a young man in his thirties wearing a three-piece Victorian-era suit and a top hat appeared to be stuck in a sideboard topped with teacups and teapots for sale.

"Not you again." I recognized the ghost of Dalton Banks, who'd materialized in my kitchen the day before asking me to find out who killed him. "I thought I'd explained that you need to look for the light. Your work here is done."

I'd also given him my firm assurance that I was retired from the business of solving murders. Even though he seemed disappointed, Dalton had blipped back out, which I'd hoped ended our acquaintance before it even began.

"Yes, about that," he said. "Can we talk?"

"Not until you remove yourself from that cabinet. You break it, you buy it."

The ghost looked down. "Oh. Sorry," he said, taking a careful step forward. The cups rattled, but nothing broke. "I'm not very good at this. Is there an instruction book or something for being dead?"

Cocking an eyebrow, I said, "How would I know? I'm alive."

He looked confused, but then said, "Oh, yeah. I forgot. Have you changed your mind about solving my murder?"

Death brings out the obstinate streak in people.

Sighing, I decided that listening to him couldn't hurt, and might even encourage Dalton to move on. "Look, I'm not promising you anything, but why don't you tell me what happened to you and why you think someone murdered you?"

Hovering in my direction, the ghost tried to sit on the sofa, only to wind up with his head and shoulders sticking out of the cushion and his backside dipped into the floorboards.

"Try standing up," I suggested. "Picture your feet on top of the floor—maybe that will help."

Disentangling himself from the cushions, Dalton arranged himself by the hearth and even held his hands out toward the flames. "I wish I could feel the heat. I'm so cold all the time."

Lack of a circulatory system will do that to a person.

While I sipped my tea, Dalton told me of the events leading to his death three days earlier. He had starred in a theatrical production of *The Importance of Being Earnest* with his fiancée Violet, directed by his best friend, Brandon Saunders. They had performed to a sold-out show on opening night.

Even before they changed out of their costumes, the triumphant cast opened a bottle of champagne to celebrate their success.

"I only drink on special occasions," Dalton said, staring into the fire. I could see the flames through his trousers and forced myself not to make mental jokes about hot pants.

"That night was so special, I gulped down my champagne," he continued. "Suddenly, my heart raced. I got dizzy, and I was shaking. That's the last thing I remember."

"It sounds like you might have had a heart attack. I know you're young, but—"

"No!" Dalton interrupted me. "I was poisoned."

I could imagine how hard it would be to accept dying so suddenly and at such a young age when you had so much to look forward to. I considered telling him so, but instead, I took a different approach.

"Who would have poisoned you?" I asked.

The hurt in his eyes put a knot in my throat. "I don't know. And I don't know why, but I know I didn't die of a heart attack or other natural causes."

"Okay." My curiosity got the better of me. "Why don't you tell me what you remember. When did you become aware you were no longer alive?"

The spirit stared at the ceiling as if trying to remember. "I woke up in the theater, but nobody would listen to me. I realized it was the next night, and I thought I'd fallen asleep and slept right through, until I heard Violet sobbing. She was crying over me."

"Violet—that's your girlfriend, right?"

"My fiancée." He smiled wistfully. "We just got engaged. I tried to talk to her, but she couldn't hear me. It didn't take long to figure out why when Brandon came into her dressing room. They talked about me being dead. I couldn't believe it at first."

"That must have been quite a shock for you."

He nodded. "She was furious with Brandon. They had a huge argument."

Interesting. "Why was she so angry?"

"Violet wanted him to cancel the evening's performance, but Brandon wouldn't hear of it. He said he'd play my part."

That seemed insensitive, considering his best friend had died the night before. Softening my tone, I said, "Do you know why he'd do that?"

"He told Violet that I would have wanted the show to go on, that I loved the theater." Dalton sighed. "He was right, you know, at least the part about loving the theater, not about the show going on."

Although I hadn't known many ghosts, I could empathize with the shock he must have felt waking up only to find out he was dead.

"That's a theater tradition, isn't it?" I asked. "Not letting anything get in the way of a performance?"

The spirit's brow creased, as if thinking cost him tremendous effort. "I guess. I can't get over the fact that one minute I was celebrating with a glass of champagne and the next I was dead."

"You said you don't drink much. Were you taking any medications?"

"Just stuff for my allergies."

"That's probably it. The alcohol interacted with your medication. I'm not an expert by any means, but if you had an undiagnosed condition, the interaction could be enough to cause heart failure. I'm so sorry, Dalton, but it sounds like you died of natural causes."

The young man's jaw set in a hard line. "It didn't *feel* like natural causes."

"I'm sure it didn't," I soothed, "but you need to

accept that you're... no longer meant for this world. There's something better waiting for you." An image of Chef alone in the kitchen for decades flashed through my head. "You don't want to get stuck here on the mortal plane for years or even decades, do you?"

"I want to get stuck long enough to find out who killed me, and I'm not leaving you alone until you help me."

He shimmered out of focus and disappeared entirely, but I had a sinking feeling I hadn't seen the last of Dalton Banks.

CHAPTER 2

I didn't have to wait long for that suspicion to be confirmed. The next morning when I stepped through the kitchen door, I jumped back in surprise. Dalton's ghostly form protruded from the sink and only his head and torso were visible.

Without bothering to offer him a good morning, I said, "Are you really comfortable having that part of your body so close to the garbage disposal?"

Dalton looked down, yelped, and leaped into the middle of the room.

That was probably a mean thing to do, but I couldn't help myself. Besides, it would be smart for him to be more aware of his surroundings.

When I saw his stricken expression, I took pity on the hapless haunt. "You do understand nothing in the human world can harm you now, right?"

"Kinda," he said, "but garbage disposals scare me, anyway."

I felt a little guilty for scaring him. "It would be

helpful for you to let go of some of your anxiety, Dalton. Your afterlife will be much more pleasant if you don't let yourself worry about things that can't harm you anymore."

He used his hand to smooth the permanent post-mortem wrinkles out of his vest. "What I'm worried about is who killed me, and I will not leave you alone until you get worried, too."

"Can we not do this until I've had my coffee?" I wasn't a morning person and preferred to have at least one cup of brew before dealing with complicated issues.

I heard a gasp from the area of the stairs and turned to see Jennifer standing on the bottom step in a pink fuzzy sweater and black and white polka dot capris holding an armful of books. "He's back! Chef came back!"

Thanks to Dalton, I now had to have a conversation with her I'd been putting off. Taking a deep breath, I said, "It's not Chef."

Her eyes went round. "Oh my God! You mean you can talk to *other* ghosts, too? When did you find out? Why didn't you tell me?"

"It's not that long ago I finally told you about Chef," I said. "You've been incredibly understanding and open-minded, but others haven't been so accepting. I figured I'd take it one ghost at a time. I didn't even know I could see other ghosts until I ran into the Amazing Kaslov's dead sister at the castle." I frowned at the memory of how unhelpful Theadora had been when I'd been held captive.

13

"That is *so* cool!" Jennifer grinned. "Is she here now?"

"No, I haven't seen her since I was rescued from the dungeon at Kaslov's castle." Gesturing toward my new ghost, I said, "Dalton Banks, meet Jennifer Skillings. Jennifer, meet Dalton."

Squinting, she said, "Hi, Dalton. Sorry I can't hear you or see you, but welcome to our home. It's very nice to meet you."

"Well," the ghost huffed, "at least *someone* in this place is friendly and has some manners."

Narrowing my eyes, I said, "Is it a good idea to insult the person you're bugging for a favor?"

"What does he want you to do?" Jennifer asked.

"He wants me to find out who murdered him, but I told him I don't do that kind of thing."

Frowning, my all-too-honest assistant said, "Since when?"

Rewarding that question with a pointed look, I said, "Since *now*. I never intended to get involved in murder investigations, but when the people I cared about were accused or in danger, I had to do something."

"Not only other people," Jennifer said. "You were in danger, too."

"Exactly." Chasing after murderers could be risky. "Why would I get involved when I don't have to? Besides, Dalton probably died of natural causes. I'm not sure why he's clinging to this plane."

Jennifer gave that some thought. "Maybe you can take a quick look into what really happened to him if that would help him make the transition."

"I like her," Dalton said with evident approval. "She's smart and nice. You should listen to her."

Resigning myself to the situation, I said, "If I listen to her and look into how you died, will you go away?"

Once again, the ghost drew his brows together as if concentrating on his answer. "I'll go away if you don't find anything suspicious."

That sounded like an opportunity too good to pass up. "Okay. I'll go upstairs to my office and see what I can find online. Maybe there's an article about your death in the local paper. I'll start there."

"You can stay right here," Jennifer said, setting her books on the kitchen island and pulling out a laptop in a sleeve that I hadn't noticed. "Use my computer while I make your coffee." With a few quick keystrokes, she called up a web browser and turned the machine toward me.

Dalton came closer to watch over my shoulder. "The theater is in Stockville. That's where I live," he explained, adding, "Well, used to live. The local paper is the Stockville Sentinel."

Although I'd never been to the central California town, I recalled reading an article in the real estate section of the Sunday paper. Stockville had been an industrial center that was enjoying a kind of renaissance, with old buildings being renovated and businesses returning to the now trendy downtown area.

The town's turn-of-the-century architecture attracted younger, more bohemian couples with money who not only pumped their dollars into the local economy, but also encouraged a kind of artsy vibe. I suspected that included support for independent theater productions like the one in which Dalton had starred.

I stopped scrolling when I found an article in the entertainment section mentioning his death.

"Listen to this," I said, and read the headline. "Beloved Actor's Light Extinguished Too Soon."

"So true," Jennifer looked over my shoulder at the article. "Read it aloud for us."

I cleared my throat and read. "Theatergoers were shocked to learn that beloved local actor Dalton Banks passed away shortly after his stellar performance as Algernon Moncrieff in 'The Importance of Being Earnest,' leaving fans and colleagues devastated."

Dalton's eyes widened. "It really says that?"

"It does." I continued reading. "Banks, known for his magnetic stage presence and dedication to the local theater community, had completed his final bow when he collapsed. Despite immediate medical attention, the young actor was pronounced dead at the scene."

Somehow, reading those words brought home the brutal truth. Even though I could see Dalton's ghost and heard him tell me about his death, it didn't seem real until I read those words.

"I'm sorry, Dalton," I muttered. "I'm sorry you had to die."

He didn't make eye contact with me, but gestured for me to keep reading.

"Banks was particularly beloved in Stockville where he and his close friend, director Brandon Saunders, had worked tirelessly to preserve the historic Elliott Palace Theater, which had been slated for demolition."

Skimming the rest of the article, which ended by saying that Dalton was survived by his fiancée Violet Roberts, my eyes lingered on a cast photo taken opening night in full costume.

Unfortunately, the photo was low resolution, and I couldn't make out much detail, but I recognized Dalton in the front row. In the row behind him, a dark-haired man glared in Dalton's direction. A trickle of suspicion started in the back left corner of my brain.

Taking another look at Dalton's smiling face, I thought about how we never know when our last day will be. I could be drinking a latte one minute and the next...

Jennifer set a vanilla latte in front of me. "Is Dalton in that picture?" When I pointed him out, she grinned. "He's very handsome."

"Thank you," Dalton said."

I glanced at the ghost, taking a better look. "Not bad looking for a young kid."

"Kid?" Dalton sounded offended. "I'm over thirty."

"That old, huh?" Anything under forty sounded young to me since I'd hit fifty last year. "I'm going to see if there's any more information online about your death."

It took half an hour before I convinced myself I'd found every bit of information that had been posted. There was a follow up article in the Stockville Sentinel that stated Dalton died of natural causes and gave details for his funeral.

I checked out the social media account for the town and the theater, but nothing contradicted the cause of death.

A wave of disappointment washed over me, and I realized I'd wanted there to be more to the story. I didn't understand why someone so young had to die, but there were so many things I didn't understand. I returned to the article with the picture of Dalton and his castmates and stared at their happy faces.

I finally gave up. "There's nothing here that makes me think your death was anything more than a terrible accident."

"Anyone in that picture might have murdered me," he said, jabbing a shaky transparent finger at the screen. "Not Violet, of course. And not Brandon. But any of the others. You've spent half an hour on the internet, and I'm supposed to accept that my death was accidental?"

"Who is that man?" I asked, pointing at the angry looking man in the second row. "He looks mad enough to..." I almost said "kill" but stopped myself and said, "spit."

"That's Brandon. He is—" He stopped himself. "He *was* my best friend." Dalton angrily stomped one foot against the tile floor. "You're no help at all."

He walked out of the kitchen and through the back door, leaving me feeling vaguely guilty that instead of helping ease his distress, I'd made it worse.

"That's not what he wanted to hear." I started to close the laptop, but instead, I returned to the photo from the newspaper article and read the caption. I got up and retrieved a notepad from the junk drawer and made a list of the names.

"Hmm…" Jennifer eyed me. "You *do* think there's something funny about poor Dalton's death."

"*Poor* Dalton?" I said, raising an eyebrow. "You can't even see him and you're calling him 'poor Dalton?' Come on, we need to finish getting ready for the day."

She watched me fold the laptop shut, put on an apron, and wash my hands.

"You are going to help him, aren't you? I want to find out what really happened to him, and I know you do too."

I didn't know any such thing, and even if I was considering doing more to ease Dalton's unhappiness, what could I do? How do you investigate a murder when everyone says there hasn't been one?

My new ghost didn't stay away for long. He spent the rest of the morning lurking by the sink while I ignored his judgmental presence and made shepherd's pies in advance of the lunch rush.

While diced potatoes boiled in my biggest pot on the back burner, I chopped and diced carrots, celery, and onions, then began browning the ground beef. As I worked, I felt a sense of comfort and satisfaction. My ancestors had made homey food like this for generations, and I loved keeping the tradition alive.

After adding the vegetables and herbs to the meat mixture, I added a little Worcestershire sauce, tomato paste, and flour to thicken the broth into a gravy. The savory smell filled the kitchen.

"That looks good," Dalton said.

I glanced up, surprised to see him still watching me. I'd gotten so involved in my cooking, I'd nearly forgotten about him. "It's one of my favorite dishes to make and to eat."

"Too bad I can't eat it," he said morosely. "Or smell it. Or taste it."

"Okay, I get it." Chef rarely complained about not being able to eat or drink the dishes he helped me prepare, and he'd devoted his life to cooking. I sighed, missing him terribly. Of course, he complained about plenty of other things, especially my cooking techniques, which he insisted needed improvement.

Jennifer popped in and out of the kitchen as she finished her own preparations for the day.

A polite knock at the back door caught my attention. I'd learned everyone's knock, from Irma's demanding rap to Freddie's firm tap-tap-tap, but I had no idea who this might be.

I found myself face to face with Sheriff Anderson Fontana—which was only possible because the six-foot-four lawman stood on the bottom step, hat in hand.

"Hi," he said with a boyish smile. "I hope I'm not interrupting." The wind ruffled his sandy-blond hair making the silver highlights glint in the sunlight.

"Of course not." I invited him in. "Is there something you need? That is, something I can do for you?" I stopped talking before I made it worse.

"I just stopped by for a chat," he said. "If you're sure I'm not in your way."

"Not at all." I gestured to one of the stools at the island. "As long as you don't mind watching me cook."

"That sounds delightful."

Jennifer pushed open the door from the front room and stopped in her tracks. I barely managed not to roll my eyes at her and waved her in.

"Hello, Sheriff." She had a "cat who ate the canary" grin. "Would you like something to drink?"

I suddenly remembered my manners. "I can make another pot of tea or coffee. You're more of a coffee drinker, aren't you?"

He didn't even get out the words, "Coffee would be nice," before I heard Jennifer working the espresso machine.

"What can I get you, Sheriff?" she said brightly. "A latte or cappuccino?"

"Which one is more like a regular cup of black coffee? I'm sort of old fashioned that way."

Giggling, Jennifer said, "I'll make you an Americano. Why don't you two sit in the front room and I'll bring it out to you."

Telegraphing a silent *"knock it off"* in her direction, I said, "I still have scones to make."

"Those take you five minutes." She spoke over the hissing machine. "You could use a break. You've been on your feet all morning."

So have you, I wanted to say, but she was a couple of decades younger than me, and a break sounded nice.

But I had an even better idea. "Why don't I show you the secret garden? It's been a passion project of mine and I'm really pleased with how it came out."

"A secret garden?"

I waited for him to make a joke, like everyone seemed to make, about it not being much of a secret.

Instead, he said, "Like the book?"

I grinned. "Exactly like the book."

Holding the door open for the sheriff, I stepped out the back door and led him along the path to my very own secret garden. I hadn't checked how the flowers were coming along for at least a week. Good thing the gardeners kept an eye on things.

At the end of the path, I pushed open the ornate gate and gazed at the delightful sight before me. The elm tree cast dappled shadows over soft green grass carpeting the ground. In the center of the garden, a fountain bubbled and gurgled, its waters sparkling in the filtered sunlight.

Sheriff Fontana leaned forward to get a look and I felt his breath on my neck. "It's beautiful," he whispered. "I wish I had a better word. It's like a fantasy world."

"Follow me," I whispered back as if we were two children sneaking into a garden that had been locked shut for years.

As I stepped carefully on the moss-covered stone path, I breathed in the fragrance of spring flowers in full bloom. Golden daffodils nodded in the soft breeze while sweet-smelling hyacinths filled the air with their perfume.

Sparrows twittered in the shrubs and a tiny hummingbird flitted from bloom to bloom. Taking a seat on a swing bench hung from the elm tree, I invited the sheriff to join me.

As the bench rocked back and forth, I listened to the birds and the tinkling of the windchimes. Everywhere I looked, new wonders unfolded, each one a testament to the power of life to reinvent itself.

We sat in silence until Jennifer appeared.

"Oh my." She stood at the gate with her mouth open in awe holding the sheriff's Americano and a latte for me. "It's changed so much in such a short time."

She remembered why she was there and handed us our coffee drinks before scurrying back to the kitchen.

I sipped my drink, feeling like I was in heaven. "Was there something in particular you wanted talk to me about?"

Taking his own experimental sip, the Sheriff's eyes widened. "This is good."

"Jennifer's a whiz with that machine. I can't make the darn thing work at all. I don't know what I'd do without her."

"Hopefully you never have to find out."

I nodded and waited to hear what he had to say.

He cleared his throat. "I need some advice."

I did my best not to look surprised. "About what?"

"Well, I was wondering if…" He stopped and tried again. "I mean how long after… When a man gets divorced…"

Taking pity on him, I asked, "Are you thinking of starting to date again?"

A faint hint of pink spread over his rugged features. "Yes."

I wanted to tell him that I'd been waiting for him to be free so he could ask me out. I'd felt a strong attraction the first time I met him, and I suspected he did too. But he was married at the time, so neither of us said a word about how we felt.

"Well?" he asked.

Rebound relationships could seem so right and be so wrong, and I didn't want to get hurt again.

I sucked in a breath and hoped I said the right thing. "There aren't any set rules about that kind of decision, but I think it's best not to get involved with someone simply because you're lonely."

"I see." Fontana waited for me to continue.

"Rebound relationships can be..." I felt funny talking to him about his love life, but I pushed on. "What I'm trying to say is they can feel new and exciting, and those feelings can cause you to overlook red flags."

The sheriff's fingers circled the rim of his cup. "So, if there's someone I'd like to get serious with, I should wait before I asked them out?"

With every fiber of my being, I hoped he was talking about me, but I swallowed that feeling and stuck to the script.

"Yes." I stared into my half-empty cup. "You've been through a lot in the last few months. I wouldn't want you to rush into anything and get hurt again."

He leaned back, causing the bench to swing again. "I don't think the lady in question would hurt me, but I suppose waiting a little while probably is a good idea."

Me and my big mouth.

"Thanks for the coffee and the advice." He stood and held out a hand to help me to my feet. "I'll let you get back to work."

As I followed him along the stepping stones, I said something completely unplanned. "Can I ask *your* opinion about something?"

The nagging possibility that Dalton could have died by foul play refused to leave me alone. Sometimes having a conscience can be a real pain in the backside.

"Sure," the sheriff said. "As long as you haven't stumbled over another dead body."

His face fell when he saw my expression. What was I going to say? *Well, I haven't actually seen the body, but the ghost is in my kitchen?*

Fontana said flatly, "You're at it again, aren't you?"

Wincing, I said, "What do you mean, *at it again*? I never meant to get involved in any of those other cases." I told myself to calm down. "And besides, it's not like that. Just hear me out."

The sheriff listened as I described the circumstances of Dalton's death. When I finished, Fontana hit me with a pointed question. "And what's your interest in all this?"

Since I didn't want to lie to a man who might, theoretically, be on my dating radar, I told him I had a friend in Stockville. Technically, it was the truth since Dalton was from Stockville, and I had started to think of him in friendlier terms. In some ways, his persistence reminded me of Chef.

"April, why don't you spend your time thinking about happier things? Here we are in this beautiful garden brimming with new life, and you're thinking about death."

"I'll think about happier things when I find out what happened to Dalton. Will you at least read the newspaper story about the incident and tell me what you think?"

When the sheriff begrudgingly agreed, we returned to the kitchen. I ran upstairs and pulled up the article on my desktop computer and printed it out. When I came back downstairs and handed him the sheets, Fontana took a pair of reading glasses out of his shirt pocket and went over the text with maddening deliberation.

"There's not one thing here to suggest this boy was murdered," he said at last, straightening the sheets and tapping them on the island for good measure. "And if he had been, Stockville has a large and capable police force to take care of the matter."

Yeah, and not even one of those cops had the advantage of being able to speak directly to the victim —but I kept that part to myself.

Seeing the look of consternation on my face, Fontana went on. "I know life around here can get boring, but you can't go looking for a murder every time someone dies. There are other ways to add spice to your life."

What was I supposed to say to that? Anderson Fontana could spice up my life anytime he wanted to, but the murder victim had come looking for me and didn't seem inclined to leave me alone.

CHAPTER 3

*A*fter the sheriff left, I managed to get my mind on business around the time the first customer walked through the door.

Over the past several months, Jennifer and I had developed a solid working routine. She served our guests while I stayed in the kitchen, putting in the occasional appearance in the front room to help out and thank people for coming.

With so many locals stopping in for lunch, we had a nearly full house. Jennifer and I both worked the crowd, filling drinks and dispensing shepherd's pie, sandwiches, and bowls of steaming soup.

During the first lull, I hastily mixed dough for more scones. While the pastries baked and a batch of mini quiches cooled on the counter, I arranged tiered trays of sandwiches.

Dalton, who had been watching us all day without comment, bent over to examine a platter of tiny desserts. "You sure don't give people very much for their money."

"*That*," I said, using a mitt to take the scones out of the oven, "is not true. Our servings are very generous. The small sandwiches and pastries allow people to try one of everything. It's much better than having to choose just one item."

"Huh," he said. "If you say so. I'm more a cheese-burger and energy drink kind of guy."

I froze with the baking sheet in mid-air. "You drank energy drinks?"

"All the time," he said. "My allergy doctor said he couldn't figure out why my blood pressure was so low with all that caffeine in my system. I guess I have good genes."

Carefully putting the hot baking sheet down, I said, "Dalton, did your doctor warn you about drinking so many energy drinks?"

The ghost shrugged. "Yeah, but it never bothered me."

"Do you understand that caffeinated drinks—especially high-powered ones—can lead to heart failure, especially when mixed with medications? The combination could be lethal for someone with a weak heart."

Glowering, he said, "Everyone in my family has always been as healthy as a horse. If it wasn't for the accident, my parents would probably have lived to be a hundred."

"You may not have known about the condition," I suggested with gentle sympathy. "The more you tell me about your life, the more I think your death was due to natural causes."

This time when he stomped his foot, Dalton drove his right leg into the floorboards up to the kneecap. Standing at a lopsided angle, the ghost said, "Someone tried to kill me. Why won't you believe me?"

"I've listened to what you have to say, but I think you're in a state of denial. You want there to be someone to blame for your death, but there's absolutely nothing that says it was murder."

"How would you know?" he fumed. "You haven't even tried to find out the real facts. You know what? I don't think that you *can* solve my murder."

Refusing to be baited, I attempted to reason with him. "Maybe you need to give some serious thought to the idea that there's nothing to be solved. Right now, I need to get back to work."

Putting on a petulant expression, Dalton said, "You're not nearly as nice as people on this side say you are."

So that's how he heard about me. I'd gotten picked up by the ghostly grapevine. Great. Did that mean more ghosts would be showing up at my tearoom, asking me to solve their murders? I certainly hoped not.

"Dalton, I know your situation is hard to accept—"

He cut me off mid-platitude. "Why don't you admit you don't care?"

And with that, he disappeared in an instant.

Even knowing that he was upset about being dead, Dalton's parting shot hurt. Was I being insensitive?

That thought nagged at me until that night when, alone in my parlor, I wondered if an obituary had been written for Dalton. Moments later, I'd found one posted earlier that day at the Stockville Sentinel's website.

I cringed when I learned his parents had died in a small plane crash when he was a young teenager. He'd experienced more than his fair share of tragedy early in life. The write-up described Dalton's love for the theater, which started when he played a tree in the first-grade play.

It takes an optimistic soul to discover his life's purpose rooted on the corner of a stage with branches sticking out of his head.

The last paragraph provided the details of the service, which would be held Saturday morning with a reception afterward at the Elliott Palace Theater in Stockville, Dalton's hometown.

Another search led me to a brief history of the theater. The building had been slated for demolition until the Revival Theater Group, headed by Dalton's friend, Brandon, had mounted a successful campaign to save it.

With a grant from a preservationist architectural foundation, the young people bought the theater and had spent the past year renovating the building, helped along by donations and proceeds generated from their productions.

Such a tragic death for someone so purpose-driven who cared so much about his community and the arts.

And too young to die. Dalton Banks wouldn't leave me alone in more ways than one.

After a night of tossing and turning, I went down to breakfast the next morning in a grouchy mood, only to be met by Jennifer, who had done some research of her own.

She greeted me at the foot of the stairs with a generous cappuccino and gushed, "Do you know Stockville was an old industrial town that was falling apart until a bunch of rich people moved in and got interested in reviving it?"

"And a cheery good morning to you, too," I said, accepting the drink. "I did know. What about it?"

My bad mood didn't faze my history-obsessed assistant.

"With the Stockville economy picking up, people are getting interested in saving the old buildings. That's what happened to the Elliott Palace Theater where…"

I finished the sentence for her. "Dalton died. I read his obituary and then I went to the theater's homepage."

That's all Dalton needed to hear to appear, but miraculously this time, he hit the middle of the room in one piece. Maybe he was getting used to being dead after all.

"The Elliott was originally a theater for workers," he said. "The owner of the biggest factory in town paid for the construction and hired an architect from San Francisco to come up with the plans. The building is one of the finest examples of Victorian design in this part of California. We couldn't let it fall apart. There are pictures on our Instagram feed of the renovations if you're interested."

I repeated his words to Jennifer. Taking out her phone, she said, "We can look at the pictures together."

I watched over her shoulder while she thumbed through the photographs. Grumpy or not, I told Dalton the truth. "You and your friends have done impressive work with the place."

Swelling with pride, he said, "We worked our back-sides off. The locals have been great about pitching in. Every detail is absolutely accurate. Brandon found an expert from the California Historical Society to help us out. She approved all the repairs and materials before the work even began."

It crossed my mind to point out that if Dalton had to die, spending his last moments alive on the stage of a building that was obviously his passion wasn't such a bad exit, but I didn't. Instead, I asked a question. "You worked on the restoration?"

"Oh yeah, and was it ever hot last summer. We don't have enough money to pay for AC yet. I thought I was going to melt. We did all our performances out back on a stage in the old parking lot with big, rented fans blowing over the crowd just to make it bearable for the audience."

"But you didn't melt?" I pressed. "No shortness of breath or chest pain?"

Something like triumph came into his eyes. "Nope. I worked circles around everybody else. I told you, there's no way I dropped dead on that stage. Not without help."

Jennifer, who wanted the information too, said, "What's he telling you?"

"That he worked in an un-air-conditioned theater in the middle of summer and the heat didn't bother him one bit. That doesn't sound like the experience of a guy with a bad heart," I admitted.

Dalton walked right into the kitchen island and planted himself in front of me. "Talk to Violet. If you don't believe me, maybe you'll believe her."

I grunted. "What am I supposed to say? 'Hello, Violet. I've been hanging out with your late boyfriend, and he asked me to call you.' That will go over well."

"Say you're my long-lost aunt or something," he suggested. "She'll tell you something's not right about my death."

I swallowed the last gulp of my now cold drink, hesitating before bringing up what was sure to be a painful subject. "Your obituary says that your parents died when you were young. What happened to them?"

Dalton got a faraway look in his eyes. "My dad had just learned to fly. He was so excited, he borrowed his instructor's plane to take Mom for a ride. I didn't go because my best friend's birthday party was that day. No one really knows what happened, but the plane crashed into the ocean."

A lump rose in my throat. Chef's reunion with Marie showed me that life's possibilities don't end with death. I knew in my heart that Dalton's parents were waiting for him somewhere, but he wouldn't be able to find them so long as he remained tied to his former life by the belief that he'd been murdered.

After I relayed the story to Jennifer, she agreed with me and asked the obvious question. "What's one phone call?"

Against my better judgement, I'd allowed myself to become invested in Dalton's story, with Jennifer along for the ride. But she was right—what could it hurt to make a phone call?

I gave in to the inevitable and grabbed my phone. "Dalton, what's Violet's number?"

The ghost performed a joyful jump that put his head right through the ceiling, but the move at least got him out of the island. Then his expression changed to a look of puzzlement.

"What's wrong?" I asked.

With a little shake of his head, he patted his jacket and then reached into his pants pockets. "I don't have my phone." He furrowed his brows, then mumbled to himself, "Of course, you don't. You're dead, remember?"

"It's okay. Maybe we can look it up," I suggested.

"It's not okay." Dalton, his shoulders hunched, stared at the ground. "Violet is my fiancée. I should be able to remember her number. Why can't I remember?"

I didn't know how to cheer up a distraught ghost. After all, I couldn't offer him a warm cup of tea or some shortbread cookies.

"Dalton, you've been through a lot recently." Boy, that was the understatement of the year. "I'm sure there are a lot of things that you don't remember from your former life, but you remember the important things, right? You remember Violet and your

34

feelings for her. So what if you forgot her number. That doesn't say anything about what she means to you."

He gave me a weak smile. "I suppose so." Then he brightened and blurted out "867-5309!"

Somehow, I managed not to laugh. "That's from a song. 'Jennie, Jennie, I've got your number' remember?"

He sighed. "Fine. Go ahead and see if you can look up her number."

Jennifer, who'd been following my side of the conversation gave me a questioning look. "Can I help?"

Within minutes, she'd found Violet's unlisted cell phone number and I made the call. A woman answered on the fourth ring.

"Is this Violet Roberts?" I asked.

"Yes," she answered in a mournful voice. "I'm not interested in buying anything."

"I'm not selling anything. My name is April May. I'm calling about... my nephew, Dalton Banks."

A hint of suspicion colored her next words. "Dalton didn't have any family."

Summoning every ounce of commiseration I could muster, I said, "That's true, sort of. I'm his aunt by marriage on his mother's side. I haven't seen him since his parents died, but I'm in Serenity Cove and I read about his death in the paper."

I held my breath. The genealogical gibberish was utter nonsense, and why would the Serenity Cove newspaper cover a death in a town three hours away?

Violet was in such a state, however, that she bought the whole story without question. A sob came over the line. "Oh, Dalton would be sorry he missed seeing you. It always bothered him that he didn't have any family."

She sounded so bereft, I tried to offer her what consolation I could. "The obituary said you were his fiancée, so really you were his family."

That set off a fit of actual crying. "Oh, Aunt April, you're so sweet. Thank you. Thank you so much. Are you coming to the service tomorrow?"

Taken aback by being called "Aunt April," I stammered, "Well, I..."

Violet dropped her voice to a whisper. "Please say you'll be there. I have to talk to someone. You're Dalton's family, so you're the perfect one to help me."

Feeling myself sinking deeper into a self-dug hole, I tried not to sound unkind. "Don't you have friends who can help you work through your grief?"

In my imagination, I could see the distraught girl looking both ways before she answered.

"Not about that," she whispered. "The police said Dalton died of natural causes, but I don't believe it. I think someone murdered him, and I'm scared I could be next."

Dalton must have overheard because what little color he had drained away to a thin gray.

"Why would you think that?" I asked.

Still whispering, she replied, "I can't tell you over the phone, but I have a good reason."

That newly discovered part of myself that loved to unravel mysteries wanted to say yes, and my heart hurt at the thought of the girl being afraid for her life. Then

I remembered Sheriff Fontana's description of the perfectly competent Stockville police department.

"Violet, tell the authorities about your suspicions and get police protection," I said firmly. "They can help you far more than I can. I'm sorry about the service, but it's almost a three-hour drive from Serenity Cove. I'll send a donation to the theater in Dalton's memory." I paused, adding, "I'm so sorry for your loss."

Even to my ears, that sounded like a pat dismissal.

"Okay," she replied, in a dejected voice. "It was asking too much to think that anyone would believe me, much less a stranger. Thank you for calling."

She broke the connection before I could say anything else.

I turned to Jennifer. "She called me, Dalton's only living relative, a stranger." I realized how silly that sounded. "I know, I know. I *am* a stranger. But she doesn't know that."

Jennifer looked at me like I'd kicked a puppy. "*April!* What is wrong with you? That poor girl is afraid for her life! Why won't you go meet her and hear what she has to say?"

"Yeah," Dalton chimed in. "Violet could be in real danger."

"I have a tearoom to run, and we need to get started on the day. The police are much more capable of handling something like this. If Violet talks to them, she'll be fine."

Why did that word "if" sound so terribly ominous?

CHAPTER 4

ll afternoon as I baked scones and stacked trays with finger sandwiches and mini quiches, my brain insisted on going back to that single idea. *"If Violet talks to the police."* The thought begged consideration of the flip side of the equation, *"And what if she doesn't?"*

As I filled teapots with hot water, I told myself she wasn't in any real danger. Dalton almost surely died of natural causes and that meant Violet's concerns were imaginary.

But what if I was wrong?

Jennifer hardly spoke to me as she came in and out of the kitchen delivering food and tea to the tearoom's guests and returning with empty dishes and cups. The accusatory looks flying at me from my new live-in ghost didn't help me feel better about my decision not to get involved.

As busy as I was baking and cleaning, I couldn't get the teary apprehension in Violet's voice out of my mind. I didn't like disappointing her—and Dalton—but I couldn't be in two places at once. As Dalton hovered nearby, he could see me taking one batch of scones out of the oven and putting another in. He had to agree that Jennifer couldn't run the tearoom by herself, and I told him so.

"You could close for a day," he said. "What's one day?"

I put my hands on my hips. "Spoken like someone who's never owned a business."

After we closed for the day, Jennifer helped with the cleanup then went up to her room. As I prepped for the next day, I carried on a running monologue. I'd gotten used to "talking to myself" when I had Chef for company, and now I couldn't stop, especially when confronted with a conundrum.

As I sifted flour to pre-mix lemon bars for the next day, I revisited my excuse for staying home. "It makes no sense to drive three hours to attend a stranger's funeral when there's no evidence suggesting he was murdered."

Dalton, who was leaning against the refrigerator with his arms crossed, said sullenly, "Keep telling yourself that."

I pretended not to hear him, but I noticed that his physical control had improved. The ghost's shoulder touched the appliance rather than melting through it. The news that his girlfriend might be in danger seemed to have galvanized Dalton into stability.

Digging in the drawer for measuring spoons, I kept talking. "It's not like I know any of these people, and the estranged aunt excuse came off as pretty flimsy."

"You know me," Dalton said, "or at least you do now. Besides, Violet believed your story. She even called you Aunt April."

Hearing him repeat Violet's words tugged at my heart. I would be an aunt as soon as my brother and Lulu's baby was born. I shook off my emotional reaction and reminded myself that I wasn't anyone's aunt yet.

When I didn't respond, he went on. "We can tighten up the details. Add in that we had a falling out after my parents died. Tell her you couldn't take me in when I was orphaned, and I never forgave you."

One look at his glistening eyes and I knew I would have never forgiven me, either. I hadn't had the most nurturing family growing up, but at least I had a mother to come home to after school.

With the dry ingredients ready, I reached for a lemon, zesting with unusual enthusiasm. Even though I didn't answer the ghost, I had to admit that his reworking of the proposed cover story would probably fly. The family falling out was an angle I could sell.

Without meaning to, I started rehearsing dialog in my head. *I'll never forgive myself for not rearranging my life and making room for that sweet boy.* If I punctuated that line with a tissue dab at a damp eye, I'd have the mourners in the palm of my hand. Oh! Maybe I could wear a hat with a veil. Then I frowned. Was a veil too last century?

I was so preoccupied, I jumped when Jennifer came

into the kitchen and proceeded to zest my own knuckles.

"Ouch!" I yelped, heading for the sink to wash off the scrapes. "See what you made me do," I accused Dalton.

Cocking her head to one side, Jennifer said, "Unless the fridge has a grudge against you, I'm guessing Dalton is still here?"

"He's here all right," I grumbled, hunting for bandages in the junk drawer. "And he's distracting me."

"I'm not doing any such thing," Dalton said. "You're distracting yourself because you know Violet's in danger and no one's doing anything about it."

The back door opened, and Irma entered with her granddaughter close behind. Zoe held Whisk cradled in her arms, which was one more problem I did not need for the day.

"No, no, no, no, *no*," I said. "The health inspector would fine the heck out of me if he found a cat in the kitchen. He might even close us down."

Looking wounded, Zoe said, "But I found Whisk outside and it's not safe for him out there. I had to bring him inside."

"Lighten up, lady," Dalton said to me. "Or do you not care about the cat, either?"

That did it. Wheeling on the carping ghost, I snapped, "Mind your own business."

Zoe froze. "Did you just chew out the refrigerator?"

"She's probably talking to a ghost," Irma said, propping her walking stick by the back door like nothing had happened.

I held my breath, but Zoe never missed a beat. "Cool. Who is it? Can they hear me?"

It would be great if everyone took the news in stride like that. A thought of Sheriff Fontana and how he might take the news flashed in my mind, but I'd have to worry about that later.

"Yes, he can hear you." I bandaged my knuckles as I spoke. "His name is Dalton Banks and I'll tell you more about him *after* you take Whisk back up to the attic. You're right that he shouldn't be outside, but he yowls to the high heavens when I close the window."

"He won't yowl if he knows I'm here," Zoe said, nuzzling the Bengal's head and kissing his ears.

I smiled despite my misgivings. "Okay. Have a talk with Whisk about that. I'll tell you about Dalton when you come back."

While Zoe ran upstairs with the cat, I looked at Irma. "Where have you been? I haven't seen you in a couple of days."

Pretending to be offended, she said, "I have other interests besides sitting around here eating your pastries and drinking your coffee."

"Do you now? So, does that mean you don't want to stay for supper? I'm making grilled cheese sandwiches and warming up potato leek soup."

A hungry look came into her eyes. "Well, I wouldn't want to be rude and refuse your hospitality."

"That's what I thought." I laughed, taking a large container of soup out of the refrigerator, and putting it in a pot to warm on the stove. After the complicated day I'd had, having friends around me felt good.

By the time Zoe rejoined us, I'd assembled the sandwiches and opened a bottle of wine.

"We're staying for supper," Irma announced as her granddaughter sat beside her. "I want to hear everything about the new ghost, too."

The girl frowned. "*New* ghost?"

Irma grinned, enjoying surprising her granddaughter. "A little while after April bought this monstrosity of a house and moved in, she started asking me questions about Chef Emile Toussaint."

"I'd found one of his cookbooks in the attic," I explained.

"That was her cover story," Irma said. "The real reason she asked about him was because she'd seen his ghost in the kitchen. I'd worked with him when I was a teenager until he kicked me out of the kitchen and the owner made me a hostess."

"Chef Emile used to call her his 'petite carotte.'" I chuckled at the memory of the look Irma gave me the first time I called her that.

"What's a 'petite carotte'?" Zoe asked.

"It means little carrot." Irma sounded proud about her nickname. "I used to steal slices of carrots after the sous chef chopped them up. I still love raw carrots. They're good for you, you know."

"I want to hear more about the chef. Is he still here?" She must have seen the look on my face because she said, "Oh, I'm sorry. Is that a touchy subject?"

I shook my head. "Not at all. He's finally enjoying his afterlife after being stuck in this kitchen for six decades."

Irma's impatience got the better of her. "What about the new ghost? Is he passing through or staying?"

"Passing through." At least I hoped so. "Dalton was an actor who died a few days ago on the opening night of his new play. He insists his death was not from natural causes, in spite of what everyone else says, and he wants me to solve his murder. It's possible that someone in the afterlife sent him my way. Like an otherworldly referral service for ghosts who think they've been murdered."

"Is that so." Irma seemed impressed that my reputation went beyond the physical realm.

Once the sandwiches were on the griddle, I related the events of the last two days, including my conversation with Violet. Jennifer chimed in from time to time with details I neglected to add, culminating in my refusal to go to the service—a fact I'd intended to skip.

"You turned the poor girl down?" Irma crossed her arms over her chest and declared, "What is *wrong* with you?"

I cringed inwardly. "I don't even know these people."

"Well, what difference does that make? That girl could be in real trouble. You've got to go to the funeral and talk to her. You might be able to help."

"Whose side are you on?" I nearly burned the sandwiches, flipping them over barely in time. "Besides, it's a long drive—too long to drive there and back in one day, especially if I'm going to spend time with Violet and the others. It would be different if I could stay the night, but that's not feasible."

"I'm on the dead guy's side," Irma replied. "How would you like to croak and be ignored in your afterlife? Or watch helplessly while your girlfriend gets killed? Exactly why isn't it *feasible* for you to go to Stockville?"

It seemed obvious to me—why didn't the others understand? "I have a business to run, if you've forgotten."

Irma rolled her eyes. "You've got Jennifer so well trained she could run this place with one hand tied behind her back. And I'm bored as heck, so I don't mind helping."

"I'll help too," Zoe volunteered. "It'll be fun."

"Oh!" Jennifer bounced up and down with enthusiasm. "If Zoe stays over tonight, I can explain everything she needs to know, and we can get to work first thing in the morning. It'll be like a working slumber party."

Zoe piped up. "And that way I can be sure Whisk stays inside where it's safe. I mean, if that's all okay with you."

Searching my repertoire of excuses, I couldn't come up with one that would survive their united front. And the more I thought about it, the more I wanted to settle the matter of Dalton's death. Besides, I could never live with myself if something happened to Violet.

Trying not to sound convinced, much less excited, I said, "Well, I guess that might work. And of course, you can stay the night, Zoe. You're invited too, Irma. Might as well make it a real slumber party."

"As long as you promise no pranks like itching powder under the covers."

I laughed. "I don't think the girls have anything like that planned." I pulled out my phone and checked the distance to Stockville. "The service is at eleven in the morning, and there's a reception afterward. I'll want to get on the road by at least seven in case I hit traffic along the way."

Jennifer gave me an impulsive hug. "I knew you'd do it. It's not like you to ignore someone in trouble. I'll be right back with my laptop, and we'll find someplace nice for you to stay tomorrow night."

Dalton's demeanor changed completely. The happy ghost began his own planning. "We can work on your cover story on the way down to Stockville, and I can coach you on the spot if anything weird comes up or if someone asks you a question you should know. By the time I'm done with you, you'll know your lines and be letter perfect."

With everyone else springing into action, Irma wasn't about to be left out. "After dinner, Zoe and I will run home and get our stuff." She seemed almost excited about the sleepover as Jennifer and Zoe.

Jennifer got me booked into the Hotel Stockville for the following night thanks to a last-minute cancellation. She showed me pictures of the historic building and rooms decorated in period style. Even if it wasn't a pleasure trip, I had to admit the pictures of the charming room with a big four-poster bed looked like a self-care treat.

The four of us, with Dalton in hovering attendance, enjoyed supper in front of the fireplace.

Zoe popped the last bite of her sandwich in her mouth. "This grilled cheese sandwich is yums. How do you make it so crispy and buttery?"

I grinned, always pleased when my food was complimented, even simple dishes. "Start with freshly baked French bread and slather on plenty of salted butter. Make sure the grill is good and hot then turn it down to medium right away. About two minutes for the first side, flip it, and less than a minute on the other side. Do that and they're perfect every time. You can make a tuna melt the same way—just add tuna salad. Obviously," I added.

Afterwards, Jennifer insisted we move to the upstairs parlor for a viewing of the 2002 movie production of *The Importance of Being Earnest* with Reese Witherspoon.

"It would be helpful for you to be familiar with the play," she said, "so you'll understand more about Dalton and what he was doing when he died."

Honestly, I only said yes because who wouldn't want to look at Colin Firth for an hour and thirty-seven minutes?

Once we got settled in with a bowl of popcorn, some homemade snack mix, and lap blankets to keep out the chill, Jennifer pressed play. The evening turned out to be fun, with Dalton critiquing every performance while I served as interpreter.

"Ah, Reese Witherspoon," he said as the opening

credits came on screen. "I loved her in Legally Blonde. Let's see if she can pull off an English accent."

"I love everything Reese Witherspoon does," Jennifer said, "but this isn't my favorite role of hers."

Moments later, Dalton's eyebrows drew together. "Starting with a chase scene? Interesting choice. Not how I would have done it, but, well, let's see where it goes."

After a few scenes, I remembered why I enjoyed the play so much. "Oscar Wilde has such a way with words, doesn't he?"

Dalton frowned. "I'm not sure these actors are doing it justice. It seems a bit flat, don't you think?"

Jennifer's eyes stayed glued to the TV screen. "It's worth watching if just for the costumes as far as I'm concerned."

After the credits rolled, I still had to pack, and I hadn't given a thought to what I would wear to the funeral. I said goodnight to the three women and told Dalton I'd see him in the morning.

"Bright and early." It occurred to me that I didn't know if ghosts slept, but I doubted it. "I'm leaving at seven a.m. with or without you, so if you want to whoosh your way there, go for it."

"Whoosh?" Dalton asked skeptically.

"I don't know the terminology for ghostly movement. How'd you get here from Stockville the first time I met you?"

Dalton concentrated, trying to remember. "I don't know."

I felt bad for the guy. He seemed lost in his new

role, but it would come to him in time, I felt sure of that.

Zoe planned to bunk in with Jennifer, while Irma took the guest room. Right before we all turned in for the night, Irma paused with her hand on the doorframe and said, "Mind if I ask a couple of people over for dinner while you're gone?"

"Not at all," I assured her. "Have a good time. I restocked the walk-in freezer last week. Use anything you like."

"Oh," Irma said, with uncharacteristic nonchalance. "I may pick up a few things on my own. I don't want to use your groceries."

By the time I found an outfit that would do for a funeral and put a few other items in my bag, I crawled into bed. I lay awake, wondering what I was getting myself into, both in pretending to be Dalton's aunt and in leaving my tearoom in the hands of Jennifer, Irma, and Zoe.

I rolled over and scolded myself for worrying. How much trouble could they get into in one day?

CHAPTER 5

My alarm went off at dawn the next morning, and I dragged myself out of bed. The sunlight glowed orange through the window. What was that saying? *Red sky at morning, sailors take warning.* Good thing I wasn't a sailor.

I had enough time for a quick shower and a few swipes of mascara before dressing. I pulled on the dark gray slacks and maroon sweater I'd selected for the service. Not the most fashionable outfit in my closet, but it was appropriate for the occasion.

When I came downstairs, Jennifer and Irma had a full breakfast of scrambled eggs, hash browns, bacon, and toast waiting for me. The aroma filled the space, making my mouth water.

"I put two shots of espresso in your cappuccino this morning." Jennifer set a steaming mug in front of me. "To keep you awake on the road."

Between the strong coffee and the delicious food, I sighed with pleasure. "You two are amazing. I can't believe you got up early to make me this wonderful breakfast."

"It's eggs," Irma said, slathering more butter on her toast than her cardiologist would like. "Any fool can make eggs."

"Then you two fools did an amazing job." I looked around, half-expecting a huge mess. "And this kitchen is spotless."

Jennifer grinned. "See. You don't need to worry about us at all."

"Apparently not," I agreed. "Where's Zoe?"

"Still in bed," Irma said. "With your cat."

That made me choke on my coffee. "Whisk slept with her?"

"Curled up under her arm," Jennifer affirmed. "He came down from the attic and scratched at my bedroom door to be let in. Then he jumped right up on the bed and curled up next to Zoe."

"Has anyone considered the possibility that Whisk might have fleas?" I asked.

"Zoe," Irma said. "She took him to the vet last week, got his shots, and some of that long-lasting flea stuff."

"When did she do that?" I wasn't the most observant person, but I think I would have noticed Zoe carrying my attic cat out the front door.

"The day you went shopping in Somerton," Jennifer said. "I didn't think you'd mind."

"Of course, I don't mind, but I'm stunned he let her take him to the vet." I'd tried to lure him into a cat carrier more than once and always failed.

Jennifer carried my dish to the sink. "I couldn't believe it either."

"She shouldn't have spent her money like that," I protested. "Whisk is my responsibility."

"I paid for it," Irma said, trying to make the admission sound gruff. "The kid loves that alley cat. Don't worry about it."

That almost made me choke on my eggs. If Irma didn't want to be reimbursed for an out-of-pocket expense, Zoe was most definitely a positive influence on her crotchety grandmother.

"Look," Jennifer said. "I took a picture of them. Aren't they precious together?"

She shoved her phone across the island. Sure enough, the notoriously stand-offish Whisk lay snuggled against Zoe, sound asleep.

"Remind her she can't take him into the kitchen or the tearoom," I warned.

"Don't worry," Jennifer assured me. "Zoe knows the rules, and really, so does Whisk. He never comes any farther downstairs than the landing."

"True," I said, gesturing toward the phone's screen, "but she's introducing him to the high life."

Dalton stuck his head through the door to the front room. "Can we please get on the road? You're going to make me late for my own funeral."

Glancing at the clock, I saw it was almost seven. I doubted we'd be late, but I didn't want to risk any unforeseen complications.

"Dalton's eager to get going. I'll report in after the

service." I gulped down the last of my coffee and set my cup in the sink.

"Wait until you get settled at the hotel tonight," Irma said. "Then you can give us a rundown on the whole day. Call when you're getting ready for bed."

I rolled my bag out to the car, stowed it in the trunk, and climbed in beside Dalton, who already occupied the passenger seat. He perched comfortably atop the upholstery and with one elbow casually leaned against the arm rest.

"You're looking unusually solid this morning," I said as I backed out of the driveway.

"I'm excited." His grin reached his eyes, crinkling the corners. "It's not every day that you get to go to your own funeral."

That was true, and most of us were unconsciously grateful.

Before I made it to the city limits, my phone rang. A glance at the caller ID told me it was Dr. Freddie Severs, the county coroner, my personal physician, and a good friend. She'd been away at a medical conference, so the opening line of the conversation startled me when I answered the phone over my car's Bluetooth speaker.

"Why am I the last one to find out there's a new ghost in your life *and* you're going to Stockville to investigate a possible murder?"

"Uh, hi. How was your conference?"

"We're coroners, so you can probably imagine. You probably would have found it a bit too gory and yet somehow boring. Tell me about the new spirit."

"His name is Dalton Banks, an actor from Stockville. He's in the car with me and can hear everything you say." I launched into an abbreviated version of Dalton's story ending with the information that his favorite meal was a cheeseburger and energy drink.

"Not the healthiest of diets, but not unusual for a young man. How old did you say he is?"

I glanced over at Dalton.

"Thirty-two," he said, and I repeated his answer to Freddie.

"Ask him how many energy drinks he usually had in a day."

"He can hear you."

"Well, fine. How many?"

Dalton shrugged and said, "Five or six. Maybe one or two extra if rehearsals ran late."

After I relayed the information, the line grew so quiet, I thought I'd lost her. "Freddie?"

"I'm here," she said. "Five or six energy drinks wouldn't normally have been enough to cause problems unless he had undiagnosed cardiac issues. The same with the allergy medication and champagne. The coroner should have been able to confirm if he had an underlying heart condition."

"Too much caffeine can be a problem though, right?"

"Definitely," Freddie agreed. "I don't recommend drinking a hundred cups of coffee, even if you have a healthy heart."

"A *hundred*?" I repeated. "No one could drink that much coffee. What about energy drinks?"

"They have about the same caffeine content as coffee. Reports of caffeine overdose are rare and usually due to people taking way too many over-the-counter diet pills."

A thought occurred to me. "What if someone slipped him extra caffeine? They could have dissolved caffeine pills and added them to his energy drinks or that last glass of champagne he drank."

"Yes!" Dalton called out. "I bet that's what happened."

I held a finger up to my lips to shush him, wanting to hear what Freddie had to say.

"Hmm…" she mulled my question over. "That could happen I suppose. Caffeine doesn't have much of a taste or an odor, but it should have shown up in the tox screen. Let me call the medical examiner's office in Stockville. I'm going to use my office phone and put him on speakerphone so you can listen in."

Beside me, Dalton said, "You know cool people. This is getting fun."

Morbid though that might have been, I'd never seen the ghost in a better mood. He might as well enjoy himself now because I felt certain he'd find his funeral more depressing than he realized.

We heard Freddie dial a number and give her name to the receptionist at the medical examiner's office. Within seconds, a man's voice said, "Freddie! This is a surprise. What can I do for you?"

"Hey, Mike. I don't mean to go poking my nose in your business, but I understand you had a young actor in your morgue a few days ago."

"Dalton Banks. What's your interest in the case?"

Borrowing my cover story, she said, "I know his aunt. She's concerned about the cause of death. I was hoping you could go over the details with me so I can reassure her."

"Well..." the man paused, and I worried he wouldn't share the information. I needn't have worried. "Since it's you," he said, "I guess it's all right. The cause of death is cardiac arrest due to ventricular fibrillation."

"I see," Freddie said, and I hoped she'd explain it to us later. "He was a young guy. Any idea what brought it on?"

"It was likely one too many of those high-powered energy drinks. It was too much for his heart."

Freddie made a sound that could have been sympathetic or disapproving. "He had a heart defect?"

"He must have," the man said. "Look, you know how backed up we get here. I did as thorough of an examination as I deemed necessary."

"Oh, sure." Freddie sounded friendly but anyone who knew her as well as I did would have heard the disapproval in her voice. "What were the levels on the tox screen?"

The M.E. rattled off some numbers and Freddie let out a low whistle. "Good Lord, Mike. He'd have to consume about fifty of those drinks to have levels like that."

A note of professional offense came into the man's voice. "Are you questioning my findings?"

"Of course not," Freddie said smoothly. "I just can't believe how young people gamble with their health."

"Me either," he replied. "I never like to say that anyone who shows up on my table deserves to be dead, but this guy brought it on himself."

Dalton sat up straighter. "*Hey!* Who does that guy think he is?"

Shushing the indignant ghost, I heard Freddie sign off the call. "You there?" she asked, coming back to us.

"We're here. Dalton doesn't think much about your colleague's bedside manner."

"That's what happens when all your patients are dead. You forget how to mind your manners around people who are still breathing. I like Mike, but he's not the most brilliant or thorough coroner I've ever met. Unless your ghost is grossly underestimating his caffeine consumption, I'm going to have to agree with him."

"Meaning?" I prompted.

"His death does not appear to be due to natural causes."

"Thanks, Freddie. I'll get back to you if I have any more questions."

"Okay. Be careful on the road and keep me updated. And April?"

"Yes?"

"If someone poisoned Dalton, they might not like you asking questions. Keep your eyes and ears open and get out of there if you sense anything wrong. Anything. Do you understand?"

After I assured her I'd be careful, and we said our goodbyes, Dalton asked, "Now do you believe me?"

"After what Freddie said, I don't think I have a

choice." We drove in silence for several minutes while I took in Freddie's words. Dalton seemed to be mulling them over as well as he sulked in the passenger seat.

It was time to narrow the suspect list. "Who could have put something in your glass of champagne?"

"It couldn't have been Violet or Brandon," Dalton insisted.

Time for a different tactic. "Why don't you tell me who was with you backstage the night you died. Violet, Brandon, and who else?"

Dalton tapped his finger against his cheek. "It's so fuzzy."

It seemed dying had done something to his memories, and I had no way of knowing if they'd get better or worse. If they were fading, then we might not have much time to find out who killed him.

I decided a change of subject would do him good, and besides, he needed to prepare me for the role of his estranged aunt. "Why don't you give me a rundown on the people I'm likely to meet at the service?"

"Well, you already know about Brandon and Violet. They both have understudies, but Brandon's wasn't there that evening. I forget why." His voice trailed off as he no doubt tried to recall hazy memories.

"Was everyone else in the cast there for the toast?" I asked, trying to get him to focus.

"I think so," he said unconvincingly. "Oh! Wait until you meet the woman who plays Lady Bracknell."

"That's the role that Dame Judi Dench played in the movie, isn't it?"

"I barely know the other actors," he continued,

getting back to the subject at hand. "Why would they want to kill me?"

I left his question unanswered for now. "What about the behind-the-scenes people?" I asked. "I'm sorry, I don't know the proper terminology."

"Sterling, the stage manager, does pretty much everything. We can't afford a big crew but there are some volunteers who help." He wrinkled his nose. "I almost forgot Kelly, Violet's understudy."

"Someone you don't like?"

He gave me a guilty glance. "She's Violet's best friend, so I always tried to like her, but I really don't. Please don't tell Violet."

"That would be a little weird if I told Violet you didn't like her best friend when I supposedly haven't talked to you in years, wouldn't it?"

He nodded. "I think I'm nervous about seeing everyone again."

"Let's get back to Kelly. Why don't you like her?"

The ghost shrugged. "There's something about her that always rubbed me the wrong way."

"Maybe she didn't like Violet spending all her time with you. It might have felt like you were taking her bestie away from her or like she had to compete with you for Violet's time. Maybe…"

"Maybe she killed me so she could have Violet all to herself?"

"It's possible."

"Now I like her even less." He scowled. "I think she should be your number one focus in your investigation. Suspect numero uno."

"Now all we need is some evidence. I'll make sure to talk to her if I can and see if anyone else is willing to tell me about her."

Dalton glanced at the navigation screen. "We'll be there soon. Let's work on your cover story."

He told me about his childhood, giving me the sorts of details that a distant aunt would know. From the sounds of things, he hadn't wanted for anything material after his parents died.

"Dalton, this may sound rude, but did you have money?"

"I'm far from rich, but I'm doing okay. My parents had life insurance and that helped get me through college. I contributed most of what was left to the theater."

Insurance. I hadn't even considered that as a motive for murder. "Did you have a policy on yourself?"

"Oh, absolutely. After the way my parents took care of me, I always made sure to keep a good-sized policy."

"Define 'good-sized.'"

"A million dollars."

That almost made me swerve off the road. "Who's the beneficiary?"

"Why, Violet, of course. Do I look like the kind of man who wouldn't take care of his wife?"

"Wife-to-be," I murmured.

Dalton sat up straight, driving the crown of his top hat into the headliner. "What's that supposed to mean?"

Not wanting to upset him, I said obliquely, "A million dollars is a lot of money."

"If you're implying Violet killed me for the insurance payout, that's nuts," he huffed. "Violet loves me. She doesn't have a mean bone in her body. Wait until you meet her in person, and you'll see what I mean. She's an angel brought down to earth."

At that moment, I heard the unmistakable sound of a tire blowing as the steering wheel lurched to the left. Swearing under my breath, I guided the car onto the shoulder, got out, and surveyed the damage. What was it with me and flat tires?

"Do you have a jack?" Dalton asked.

"I've never changed a tire in my life and I'm not starting now," I replied, taking out my phone and calling roadside assistance.

After going through the menus and finally reaching a person, my heart sank when the operator told me the tow truck driver wouldn't reach us for an hour. Dalton almost lost his mind at the news.

"You have *got* to be kidding me," he yelled. "Just change the tire yourself so we won't be late."

"Dalton," I said evenly. "I would appreciate it if you didn't raise your voice to me. I'm doing all of this for you as a favor. I don't work for you."

Making a visible effort to regain his composure, he said, "I just don't want to be late. Besides, everyone knows how to change a tire."

"I don't, and even if I did, I don't want to show up at your funeral filthy and greasy. Be patient. It'll all work out."

While we waited, Dalton sulked, pacing along the side of the road. I couldn't help but wonder if Dalton's temper might have been what got him killed.

"Dalton?"

He sighed. "I'm sorry I got mad. I'm just frustrated."

"Do you get frustrated a lot?" I asked. "Or did you when you were alive?"

"What are you getting at?"

I hoped he didn't lose his temper again. "Was there anyone you butted heads with? Maybe someone who was angry because they didn't get their way? How about whoever wanted to tear down the theater? It must have been a fight to keep that from happening."

"It sure was." Dalton seemed to brighten at the memory. "It was a local development company that was supposed to get the contract from the city to redevelop that part of downtown. I met with city leaders until they were sick of me and showed up with half the town at the city hall meetings."

"They must have been pretty angry when you kept them from getting that contract."

He grinned. "They sure were. I felt like David besting Goliath with a slingshot. But it wasn't just about me." His grin faded. "Are you thinking they might have gotten rid of me out of revenge? I don't know, April. It's been years."

"Even so, they say revenge is a dish best served cold."

CHAPTER 6

We ultimately arrived at our destination, but by the time we reached the funeral chapel, had Dalton not been dead already, I would have killed him.

The restless spirit complained throughout the tire change, urging me relentlessly to tell the tow truck driver to hurry up, which I refused to do.

After listening to a lecture from said driver on getting the flat repaired and exchanged for the spare as soon as possible, we took off for Stockville again, while my ghostly passenger carped about my insistence on driving the speed limit.

"If I get pulled over, we'll never make the service on time," I said. "Besides, you don't have to ride with me, you know. Just go on to the funeral and I'll catch up with you."

Blowing out a disgusted breath, he said, "I don't know how to move around from place to place like that. Every time I try to go to Stockville, I always wind up back with you."

Just my luck. Chef and I had never discussed afterlife navigation because he never went anywhere. But, like Dalton, he did come in and out of visibility. Intrigued, I said, "When you disappear, where do you go?"

Dalton shrugged. "Nowhere until I'm somewhere again."

The ghost clearly had no better answer for me. When I pulled off the highway at the turn for Stockville, Dalton grew agitated, bouncing in his seat in his eagerness to reach the service and see Violet again.

It appeared the service had already ended when I parked the car and got out. A line of people filed past a couple standing at the door.

"Dang it!" Dalton said. "We missed that whole thing."

"Calm down. Funerals aren't any fun anyway." I eyed the attendees. "We can still talk to people like those two."

"That's Brandon and Violet talking to everyone."

By "everyone" he meant the fifteen or twenty people who had come to pay their respects. As we started toward the building, I gave Brandon a good once over.

The guy was a dead ringer for Snidely Whiplash, the classic villain from the old Dudley Do-Right cartoons, right down to the jutting chin, moustache, and dark hair. All he needed was the top hat and elongated nose to fit the stereotype of a ready-made bad guy. He wrapped his arm possessively around Violet's waist.

Violet, on the other hand, surprised me. From Dalton's description, I envisioned a willowy beauty with an ethereal air. Instead, the woman standing beside Brandon was short and plump, but with a sweet face made blotchy from extended crying.

In my preoccupation, I almost ran into a woman in her forties with salt and pepper hair headed for the parking lot. She wore a navy blue pantsuit and running shoes.

"That's Kelly," Dalton hissed as she hurried past us.

Working on impulse, I stopped her. "Excuse me. Is this the service for Dalton Banks?"

"It was," she said. "The funeral's over. Who are you?"

Surprised by her abruptness, I said, "I'm Dalton's Aunt April. I had car trouble on the way here and was afraid I would miss the service."

"Dalton's aunt?" Kelly said skeptically. "Dalton said he didn't have any family."

"It's complicated," I demurred. "Were you and my nephew friends?"

"Hardly," she snorted. "Dalton only tolerated me on account of Violet. He didn't like me much."

Interesting. Apparently, Dalton didn't hide his feelings as well as he thought. Normally the ghost might have said something, but he stood rooted in place staring at Violet and not listening to us at all.

"Oh," I told Kelly. "I'm sure that's not true. Dalton got along with everyone."

"Yeah, right. That shows how well you knew your

nephew," she snorted. "I need to get over to the theater to get everything ready for the reception. Since you missed the funeral, you might as well join us. We can talk more there. Sorry, but I need to get going."

She strode away and I watched the last of the mourners exiting the funeral home as I approached Brandon and Violet. Before I reached the top step, Brandon whispered something in Violet's ear, then ducked inside.

"Violet?" I said, extending my hand. "I'm Dalton's Aunt April. Please forgive me for missing the service. I had a flat on the way here."

Without saying a word, the girl threw herself into my arms and started to sob. "Oh, thank you, Aunt April. Thank you so much for coming."

Beside me, Dalton said, "See? I told you. She's an angel. And so sensitive. She even cries over greeting card commercials."

When I finally managed to extricate myself from Violet's soggy embrace, I saw that even though the girl's appearance was average at best, she had captivating pale green eyes and a warm smile.

"I probably shouldn't have done that," she said with disarming charm. "Dalton always told me I'm a good actress because I can access my feelings so easily, but I kind of ambushed you."

Sad occasion or not, I couldn't keep myself from smiling. "That's okay. Funerals make everyone emotional."

"Ask her about her ring," Dalton prompted. "I

bought it for her at an antique shop and she said it's the prettiest thing she's ever seen."

Glancing down, I let out a fake gasp at the large amethyst on her left hand. Diamonds encircled the purple stone in a vintage setting.

"Oh, my heavens," I said, wincing a little at how old-maid-aunt like that sounded. "Is that your engagement ring?"

"Yes," she said, holding out her hand and fighting off a fresh wave of tears. "Isn't it beautiful? I'll never take it off. As long as I wear it, I'll have a part of Dalton with me."

"I feel terrible that I didn't reconnect with Dalton before all this," I said, waving a vague hand toward the chapel. "Now I'll never be able to mend our relationship. You know, I wanted to take him after his parents died, but I… I just couldn't."

At that last, I managed to make my voice break. I felt proud of my acting abilities, but ever-the-critic, Dalton said, "You're laying it on a little thick, aren't you?"

As I dabbed at my eyes with a tissue, a deep male voice demanded, "Who are you?" Brandon had re-joined us, and he took his place next to Violet.

Violet scowled at him. "Don't talk to Aunt April like that! I told you about her."

"You told me she wasn't coming," he replied. "Why is she here now?"

"I was able to make some last-minute arrangements so I could come pay my respects to my nephew," I said, letting a hint of ice come into my voice. "And who are you?"

"Brandon Saunders," he said, sticking out his hand. "I'm just being protective of Violet. She's been through a lot these past few days and I don't want anyone bothering her."

"Of course," I said. "But I assure you that I would never do anything to make this situation harder on Violet."

Hugging my arm, Violet said, "Of course you wouldn't. You're coming back to the theater for the reception, right?"

"Your friend Kelly mentioned it to me," I said, still watching Brandon. "I'd very much like to see where Dalton spent so much time, if it's okay."

"It's absolutely okay." Violet's smile was kind and melancholy, not surprising under the circumstances. "We wouldn't have it any other way. Everyone will be there, and they'll love meeting you. Won't they, Brandon?"

"Sure," he said, putting on a smile that looked genuine enough. "How long has it been since you've seen Dalton?"

Even if I had taken an instant liking to Violet, I reminded myself that either one of them could be a murderer. His question felt like a test. "A few months before his parents died..." I started.

Dalton jumped into the breach in the nick of time. "Tell them you came to my Eagle Scout ceremony."

"When he became an Eagle Scout..."

"I was the youngest in my troop to ever get Eagle Scout at fourteen."

"He was so proud to get the award at such a young age. I think he was, what?" I pretended to search my memory. "Fourteen?"

That touched off a fresh outburst of tears from Violet. "He told me about that on our first date."

Brandon looked uncomfortable. "Why don't we all get to the theater?" he suggested. "You can tell us more stories about Dalton there, *April*."

Something about the way he emphasized my name made me dislike Brandon even more.

"I'd love to," I said. "Thank you for the invitation."

"Follow us," Violet said. "We're in the blue Prius. We're parked around back, so we'll just be a minute."

Brandon guided Violet to the car, his hand on her back. They seemed awfully chummy, but I chose not to say that out loud in case it would upset Dalton.

On the way back to my car, my new ghost friend was uncharacteristically silent. He watched Violet until she disappeared around the corner with Brandon.

Trying not to jump to snap conclusions, it crossed my mind that the person Dalton should have disliked in life might have been his so-called best friend Brandon, not Kelly.

During the short drive to the theater, however, the ghost's mood brightened. His head swiveled back and forth as he pointed out buildings up and down Main Street.

"That's the new library," he said, indicating a former

Victorian home complete with a steep roof line, turrets, and gables. "Isn't the paint job something?"

It was something, all right. To bring the old house back to its "painted lady" glory, whoever oversaw the renovation chose to go with a tri-color paint scheme dominated by cake icing pink and garish orange.

"The books are on the first two floors," Dalton said, "and there's a reading room on the third floor. Oh, and look at the store fronts. I wish my folks could have seen this."

"I guess the town was pretty run down when you were a kid?"

"It was awful. My mom used to look at the old buildings and dream about what they once were and could be again. Dad always said when he got enough money, he'd buy one of them for her. I think they'd really like what we've done with the theater."

Up ahead, I saw the blue Prius slow and pull into a parking spot in front of a period structure that put all the others in town to shame. With Jennifer and her Jane Austen obsession, I had come to have a passing acquaintance with Georgian architecture, which depended on squares or rectangles and emphasized symmetry. The Victorians showed far less restraint.

Like the library we'd passed on our drive down Main Street, the roof of the Elliott Palace Theater pitched at a precipitous slant. Any unfortunate soul who took a fall or a slide from those heights would either wind up impaled on a finial or slam into a painted iron railing.

The building, with its twin octagonal towers

flanking the stone steps, reminded me of a church gone mad. There's no doubt Dalton worshipped at its feet. "Do you know that Dame Ellen Terry played this theater?" he asked in a reverent whisper.

"Who?"

He looked at me with a horrified mixture of astonishment and pity for my ignorance. "*Dame Ellen Terry.*"

When saying the words louder and slower didn't help me clue in, he sighed. "Dame Ellen was only one of the shining lights of the Victorian theater. She lived from 1847 to 1928 and was renowned for the depth of feeling she brought to her most famous roles: Portia in *The Merchant of Venice* and Beatrice in *Much Ado About Nothing.*"

I didn't have the heart to tell him I'd narrowly missed failing my elective college theater appreciation class because I kept falling asleep. "I guess her being here was a big deal?"

"It was a huge deal. She toured the whole country. Can you just imagine someone that talented and beautiful coming here? I wish I could have seen it. We picked *The Importance of Being Earnest* for the grand reopening of the main stage because it's from the right period, but the play is also funny, so people still get it."

On the word "people" he gave me a pointed look as if I belonged to the tribe of theatrical philistines. I let it slide because Brandon and Violet had appeared on the sidewalk outside, and I didn't want them to see me appearing to talk to myself.

Getting out of the car and approaching the duo, I said, "This is even grander than the web page makes it look. You must be so proud of what you've accomplished here."

"We are," Brandon said. Even though he'd used an inclusive pronoun, why did I feel he was taking all the credit for the transformation of the Elliott himself?

"If you think this is grand," Violet gushed, "wait until you see the lobby. It was Dalton's pet project and now…" She swallowed hard. "Now I guess it will be kind of like his monument."

"What did I tell you?" Dalton asked, looking at her with adoring eyes. "She's the most perfect woman who ever lived."

Or the most gullible.

ollowing Brandon and Violet up the steps, I allowed myself to be led into a cavernous two-story lobby. Twin staircases ascended to the mezzanine on both sides, their banisters polished to a high shine. A huge fireplace dominated the far wall surrounded by ornately carved paneling.

Stained glass complimented the lead-paned windows while the biggest Persian rug I'd ever seen protected the parquet floor. Throw in decorative wallpaper, and the effect should have been garish, but instead the space conveyed a grandeur I'd rarely seen.

A knot of people gathered in front of the fireplace, which held a small but cheering blaze. I spotted Kelly laying out sandwiches on one of the refreshment tables while a dark-haired man Dalton identified as Sterling Wilson, the stage manager, circulated with an open bottle of champagne. His pale, babyish face sported a neatly trimmed beard. Thick brows perched like caterpillars above his dark eyes.

"There's something about Sterling." Dalton scrunched up his face. "Something to do with the play."

I held my hand in front of my mouth so no one would wonder why I was talking to myself. "He's the stage manager for the play, so I have no idea what you're getting at."

"Not our production, the plot of the play by Oscar Wilde. Have you seen it performed?"

"Years ago." I remembered it being quite funny with lots of mistaken identity sort of humor. I vaguely remembered an important plot point. "Was Sterling left in a handbag as a baby?"

"Very funny." Dalton gave me an annoyed look.

Sterling brought me a champagne glass, and as he filled it, he introduced himself. "Were you a friend of Dalton's?"

I did my best to give him a sad smile. "I'm his aunt, April May." Before he could tell me he'd never heard about me, I added, "We'd lost touch over the past several years. I wish I'd made more of an effort to see him while he was still alive. You always think you have plenty of time. Until you don't."

"So true," Sterling nodded. "He was a great guy. A rising star."

"Really? I got the impression he was content with his life here and his work with the theater. Did he have other ambitions?"

"He was approached by an agent from L.A." Sterling motioned to the bottle in his hand. "I'd better get back to my pouring duties. Nice to meet you."

Violet watched me staring at the bubbles dancing in

my flute. "We wanted to make today a celebration of Dalton's life and everything he meant to all of us. Champagne is for celebrating, right?"

Never mind that the last time Dalton drank champagne, it killed him.

Touched by the anxiety in her voice and the desire for approval in the words, I impulsively gave her shoulder a squeeze. "It's perfect. I know Dalton would appreciate everything you've done to honor his memory."

"I do appreciate it," the ghost croaked, tears shining in his eyes. "I just can't believe this is all for me."

Violet led me over to the buffet where I filled my plate with sandwiches, fruit, and a few scoops of a potato casserole that looked delicious. Breakfast was a long time ago and I eagerly dug into the food.

"What are these potatoes?" I asked Violet between forkfuls. "They're creamy and cheesy and... are those corn flakes on top?"

Violet nodded. "My mom always called them funeral potatoes. They're perfect for any kind of potluck, and Dalton used to love them, so..." She sighed. "I never thought I'd be making them for his funeral."

Maybe this wasn't the best time to ask her for the recipe.

When she excused herself saying she needed to powder her nose, Kelly approached me.

"Hi again," she said. "I hope I wasn't terribly rude earlier. I had to tend to a crisis at my coffee shop *and* get here to make sure the refreshments were set out. I was in a mood. Can we start over?"

I returned her smile. "Don't worry about it. It's nice of you to do this for Violet and the cast."

"Oh, I'm part of the cast. I have a small walk-on role and I'm Violet's understudy."

"I didn't know." I nibbled at a sandwich and hoped she'd fill in the silence while I chewed.

"Everyone has at least two jobs around here," Kelly said, fiddling with the floral arrangement on the table. "The cast members help with the sets or props or costumes, and volunteers take care of almost everything else. We're on a tight budget, but we've made a success out of the theater. Brandon has a producer coming in next week specifically to see Violet perform. He's been managing her career for the last few months."

"That's generous of him." To see her reaction, I added, "They seem close."

Kelly smirked. "Yeah, you're not wrong about that."

"What does that mean?" Dalton asked, but I ignored him.

Across the room, Violet sat against the wall, looking forlorn. Sterling, the stage manager, brought her a plate of sandwiches and stood by her chair as if waiting for her next command. She gave him a grateful smile.

Kelly followed my gaze. "It's hard to miss, isn't it?"

"You mean that the stage manager has a crush on Violet?"

"Who doesn't?" She smirked. "Violet never suffered

76

from a lack of male attention. But that's not what I was getting at."

As I watched, Brandon appeared, taking a seat next to Violet. He put an arm around her shoulder and said something to Sterling. The stage manager scurried off.

"I meant the way Sterling grovels. He's that way with Violet and Brandon, and he used to fawn over Dalton too. I'm sure he's hoping if one of them has a big break that he can…" She stopped mid-sentence and her face fell. "Look out. Edna's on her way over here."

"Who's Edna?" I asked, before spotting a roundish, officious looking woman marching across the lobby.

"Good afternoon, Kelly," the woman said in an exaggerated English accent. "You've done an outstanding job organizing this funerary soiree. Poor, dear Dalton would have been touched by this hint of fashion attached to his otherwise ordinary demise."

Something told me that any demise that didn't involve dueling pistols would be ordinary to Edna.

She held out a chubby hand to me, "Edna Lovelace. And you are?"

"Dalton's aunt, April May."

"Oh, my dear. Dreadful business. Simply dreadful. To lose a bright and shining light of the theater at so young an age. Please accept my condolences, and apologies. I simply came to compliment Kelly before retiring. I must rest before our next rehearsal."

As she swished away, I said, "Let me guess, Lady Bracknell?"

Kelly laughed. "Yes. Edna's a method actor. She

never breaks character. Let me introduce you to some of the less flamboyant members of the cast."

Following her into the center of the lobby, I made small talk with Dalton's castmates, smiling, and nodding at their words of sympathy when they found out who I was supposed to be.

Even though we missed the formal funeral, I was pleased that Dalton, who kept a few paces behind me, had an opportunity to hear the genuine expressions of sorrow over his death. It didn't take long, however, for the well wishes and glowing remembrances to overwhelm his fragile emotions.

Coming up to my elbow, he said, "You're doing great, but I need to be by myself. I'm going to spend some time in the auditorium."

Raising my glass to my lips to hide my reply, I whispered, "Don't you *dare* leave me alone with these people. What if I blow my cover?"

"You won't," he said, thinning to a mere wisp. "You're a natural actor. I'm sorry, April. I can't do this anymore." He turned and walked toward a set of double doors. He stopped and reached out as if to grab the handle. When his hand went right through it, he walked through the door instead.

Champagne notwithstanding, the morose mood in the lobby started driving people away after half an hour or so. When I spied Brandon heading for the men's room, I seized the chance to get Violet by herself and asked for a tour of the building.

When she suggested we start in the auditorium, I almost said we should give Dalton his privacy, but since that revelation wasn't an option, I hoped the ghost would forgive the intrusion. After all, unless he either accepted he'd died of natural causes or I solved his murder, he faced an eternity of alone time.

Just inside the auditorium, I touched Violet's arm. "When we spoke on the phone, you felt that you might be in danger. Have you spoken with the police?"

She let out a sad little laugh. "Brandon helped me see that I was getting worked up over nothing. I think when you work in the theater it's easy to be, well, dramatic."

I smiled. "That sounds perfectly reasonable." Except for the fact that I believed her fiancé's death wasn't due to natural causes. "I'm glad you're doing better. I've been worried about you."

"You're so kind." She wiped her eyes with a soggy handkerchief. "I hope Dalton knew how many people loved him. I mean, I told him every day, but everyone thought he was so wonderful."

Everyone? I nearly asked but held my tongue.

As she told me more about the theater, Violet led me down the central, red-carpeted aisle.

A lone bulb stood on a stand in the center of the otherwise dark stage.

"What is that for?" I asked.

"That's a ghost light," she explained. "Every theater leaves one light on to guide the ghost or ghosts that haunt the building."

Great. More ghosts. "The theater is haunted?"

She took my arm as we ascended a set of side steps onto the stage. "A lot of people think so. Sometimes, I hear strange noises when I'm alone in my dressing room late at night. Dalton always said there was no such thing as ghosts."

That was ironic considering his current status. "You think otherwise?"

She gave one shoulder a halfhearted shrug. "It doesn't make sense to me that we just stop existing after we die." She sighed softly. "I wish Dalton's ghost was here."

Dalton appeared a few feet away from us, intently watching his fiancée. "I wish you could tell her I am here."

"What would you want to say to him if he were?"

Her mouth tightened with emotion. "That I'll never, ever forget him. Never."

The stage was arranged for the first act of the play, and a single red rose lay on the wooden boards.

"That's where Dalton collapsed." Violet choked back a sob. "He always loved the spotlight. I mean, not in an arrogant way, but because he felt connected to the audience. He came to life when the curtain went up."

"That must be what made him a good entertainer. Caring about the people who sit out there." Gazing out at the rows of empty seats and the circular balconies, it struck me how much bravery performing must require.

She followed my gesture toward the auditorium. "Dalton cared about all kinds of people. Would you like to see his dressing room?"

"Very much."

As she held back the heavy curtain, Violet explained that the players with major parts each had private dressing rooms, while the supporting members of the cast shared separate areas for men and women.

When I stepped over the threshold into the last room Dalton had inhabited in life, my throat knotted, and a tear rolled down my cheek before I could stop it.

Dalton materialized beside me. "I didn't know it was my last day," he said in a thick voice, "or I would have appreciated it more."

Violet put her arm around me in a quick hug. "I can see you're upset. I'll give you a few minutes alone to say your goodbyes."

After she left, I wandered around the tiny room, trailing my fingers over items Dalton had left behind— a dog-eared script, a jar of face cream, and a framed photo of Violet. He'd tucked a card into the corner of the mirror. In spidery script I made out, "Break a leg, dear."

"That's from the librarian," the spirit said. "She let us use the third floor for read-throughs until we got enough areas repaired here to have real rehearsals."

"And the flowers?" I asked, gently touching the petals of a wilting rose.

"From Violet. We always gave each other a dozen red roses before every opening night performance. It was our special tradition." Dalton reached out to touch one of the blooms, but his hand went right through it. "I keep forgetting I can't touch things. It's unsettling."

"You'll get used to it."

"I'm going to see Violet." The ghost reached for the doorknob, letting out a grunt of frustration before walking through the door. He'd get the hang of it eventually.

I took a seat at the dressing table, happy to have a few moments alone to let my thoughts settle. Movement in the mirror startled me and I jumped and turned around to see the ghost of a young man wearing a pin striped suit and a wide, red tie with matching pocket square. His slicked-back hair revealed a prominent widow's peak and his piercing blue eyes seemed to look right through me. Despite his ghostly appearance, he exuded the confidence and charm of a lead actor.

"Let me guess," I said to the spirit. "You performed in Guys and Dolls the night you died."

"Hey, you can see me?" he called out to someone. "Hey, Pearl. This dame can see me."

A blonde with a chic, bobbed hairstyle shimmered into view. Her slender frame was draped in a fringed dress that swayed elegantly as she moved creating an otherworldly effect. She was the picture of elegance until she spoke.

"You kidding me?" Her voice, loud and boisterous, caught me off guard. "Hey, lady. Whatcha doin' here? You didn't come to exercise me or nothin' did ya?"

The male ghost snorted. "It's exorcise, Pearl. Ex-OR-cise. You're already in great shape." He gave her an appreciative once over.

"I'm not in the exorcism business. My name is April." It seemed only polite to introduce myself. "I'm here on behalf of another ghost who wants me to solve his murder."

"In that case, nice to meet you." She gave me a little curtsy. "I'm Pearl, and this here's George."

"You talking about the new ghost?" George asked. "I hope he's not planning on making time with my girl." He wrapped an arm around her waist and gave it a little squeeze. "Hey, I just thought of something. When you get done figuring out who killed him, maybe you can solve my murder."

Pearl smacked his arm. "We already know who killed you, you big lug."

"We do?" His brows pulled together. "Who?"

"Me, silly!" She turned to me to explain. "I thought he was foolin' around with Darla, so I threatened to kill him. Very dramatic and everything. I figured if I scared him a little, he'd knock off his philatering."

"I think you mean philandering," I suggested.

"Yeah, that's the word."

George frowned. "So, how'd I end up dead?"

"I'm gettin' to that part. See, I held the gun like this." She demonstrated with her hands held like a pistol, "but he laughed. Can you believe it?"

"You shot me?" George bellowed. "You shot me?"

"Who's tellin the story here?" She looked around as if she'd forgotten where she was. "Anyways, I cock the gun—it goes click-click—and he's *still* laughing. I guess it just made me so mad I squeezed the trigger." She sidled up to George and cooed, "I didn't mean to do it. Really, I didn't."

"I guess it's kinda my own fault for laughing. And for fooling around with Darla."

I'd seen some dysfunctional relationships, but this one took the cake. "So, Pearl. How'd you end up dead?"

"Gee. I wasn't gonna go to jail for murder! So, I shot myself."

"I see, and—"

Before I could finish my sentence, a man's voice cried out from the direction of the stage. I moved toward the sound, only to find Brandon helping Sterling up from the floor of the auditorium. The few remaining mourners in the lobby burst through the doors at the back, and Violet appeared from the wings.

"What happened, Sterling?" she cried, hurrying to his side. "Are you hurt?"

Now upright, Sterling gingerly leaned on his left leg, only to wince and pull back. He took a couple of limping steps. "I'm fine. I don't know how that happened."

"You'd think a stage manager would know where the edge of the stage was," Brandon joked. The sarcastic tone of the remark hit me wrong.

Sterling forced a laugh, though he clearly didn't appreciate the comment.

"I have an elastic bandage in my dressing room," Violet said. "Sit down and I'll wrap that ankle."

Brandon grudgingly helped Sterling hop over to a seat in the front row, before walking away. Violet reappeared and while Sterling loosened the laces on his shoe, I heard him tell her, "That was no accident. Someone shoved me."

He spotted me hovering nearby and clammed up.

"Make an excuse to go out to the lobby," Dalton said. "Sterling will start talking again once you're gone."

"Would you like something to drink?" I offered. "Water?"

"That would be nice, thank you," Sterling said. "I'm a little shaken up."

When I reached the back of the auditorium, I picked up the low pitch of Sterling's voice confiding in Violet. Trusting Dalton to get the details, I approached the refreshment table where Kelly and Brandon stood talking.

It seemed like a good time for some subtle sleuthing. "I offered to get a glass of water for Sterling. Did either of you see what happened?"

"What difference would it make?" Brandon asked. "It was an accident. If you'll excuse me, I need to see if everything's ready for our next performance."

As he stalked off, Kelly said, "Don't mind him. He may not seem like it, but he's taking Dalton's death hard. We were here in the lobby talking when Sterling yelled. Brandon ran in to see what was wrong."

Kelly filled a glass for me from a pitcher on the table and I returned to the auditorium to find Sterling easing a sock over his bandaged ankle with Violet's help. Dalton hovered behind them.

Sterling accepted the water with thanks before asking Violet to help him backstage. Once they were out of earshot, I turned to the ghost. "What did you find out?"

"Not much. Sterling was replacing one of the foot-lights when someone came up from behind and shoved him. Those bulbs are expensive, so he was more worried about trying to save the one in his hand. When he hit the floor, he looked up and the stage was empty."

Knowing that I was treading on thin ice, I asked, "Where was Violet when she heard Sterling shout?"

Dalton gave me a disapproving frown. "Don't you start talking like that again. I told you there is absolutely no way Violet would hurt me or anyone else. She said she was in her dressing room and that's that."

In her dressing room. Alone. With no alibi.

CHAPTER 8

*A*fter Sterling's accident, the remaining guests excused themselves, leaving only a few cast members to sit around the lobby and reminisce about Dalton. Attending the funeral as a spy was one thing, but it felt wrong to stay.

"I'm going to excuse myself," I told Violet. "It's been a long day. I want to get checked into the hotel and process everything."

"Oh, of course you do. I understand. Let me walk you out."

Outside, she said, "Please don't leave town without seeing me again. Promise?"

"I promise, but I'll have to get back to Serenity Cove tomorrow. I'll call you in the morning."

Giving me a warm hug, she whispered against my ear, "Thank you for coming and for being so kind to me."

Through the open lobby entrance, I saw Brandon

watching us, which I didn't like one bit. He kept staring at me until Violet went inside and closed the door.

Dalton, who was standing in one of the windows, made a series of hand gestures telling me he planned to stay, which came as a relief. Even if there were a murderer in that lobby, they couldn't hurt Dalton. And he deserved to have time with his friends in a familiar setting. The experience might help him move on.

I drove alone to the Hotel Stockville, a wonderful vintage stone building with "1910" set in the front façade in limestone blocks. At the desk, the clerk, who appeared to be in her early sixties, took my credit card.

As she processed the payment information she asked, "What brings you to town?"

Sticking to my cover story, I said, "My nephew's funeral. He died a few days ago at the theater."

Her eyebrows shot up. "Dalton was your nephew?"

"Yes. I hadn't seen him in years. We drifted apart after what happened to his parents. It breaks my heart that he died before we could make our amends."

She handed me back the card. "I am so sorry for your loss. Dalton and his friends have done the most remarkable work with that old theater. Without them, it would have been destroyed. His mother would be so proud, and I know you are, too."

Still struggling with imposter syndrome, I said, "Yes, very. Does the hotel have a restaurant? I don't feel up to getting back in the car to get dinner."

Handing me a room key straight out of the last century, she said consolingly, "After the day you've had, I bet you also need some peace and quiet. How about I have room service bring you a tray? The special tonight is herb roasted chicken with asparagus in aioli sauce, roast potatoes, and a green salad garnished with blueberries. We have Black Forest cake for dessert. How does all that sound?"

"Like pure heaven."

"Good." She gave my hand a pat. "Give the kitchen about twenty-five minutes."

When I crossed the lobby, an actual bellman opened the ornate doors of the antique elevator and operated the mechanism that took the lift to the fourth floor. He offered to carry my luggage, but I assured him I'd be fine.

Locating my room on the building's front corner, I stepped inside and was immediately transported back in time. A marble fireplace with an arched opening occupied the wall to the right side of a four-poster bed. A mirror with a gilded frame hung over the mantel.

The walls were painted in alternating panels of mossy green and cream white. A mahogany corner wardrobe sat between the two windows and twin easy chairs created a cozy nook with a view of Main Street.

The claw-foot tub in the bathroom almost made me swoon with delight. A long hot soak sounded like the perfect antidote for the day's stress and hectic pace. The desk clerk had been right. I did need an evening by myself to enjoy dinner and a bath.

The down time would put me in a much better frame of mind to get back to work on Dalton's case in the morning. The ghost, however, had other ideas.

I'd just licked the last bit of chocolate off my dessert

fork when Dalton walked through the door and, without a word of greeting, announced, "Whoever killed me tried to kill Sterling, too."

Without bothering to hide my annoyance, I asked, "Have you ever considered knocking? And I thought you didn't know how to go anywhere but my house."

The questions seemed to genuinely confuse him. "Why would I knock when I can walk through walls? And I don't think it's your house I can always find, I think it's you."

Not the most encouraging answer I've ever received.

Sticking to the main issues, I said, "Why would you knock? Because I'm entitled to my *privacy*. How would you have felt if you'd come in here and found me naked?"

The spirit's eyes almost bulged out of his head. "*Oh!* I didn't think about that."

"Obviously. Next time find a way to announce yourself," I said crossly. "And as for your theory, what happened to Sterling wasn't an attempted murder. The worst that might have come of that fall was a broken leg."

"That's not true," he said. "Sterling told Violet he found a note on his desk telling him to keep his mouth shut about what he knows. Getting pushed off the stage was a warning."

That bit of information might change things, but it didn't tell a complete story. "Okay. What does Sterling know?"

Dalton shrugged. "I have no idea. Isn't finding that out your job?"

Since I didn't get paid to solve murders, I liked the way people referred to these spontaneous investigations as my "job."

"Did you learn anything else back at the theater?"

"Yeah, Kelly finally admitted to Violet that she never liked me. That puts her at the top of the suspect list. She didn't want me to marry her best friend, so she got rid of me."

Pinching the bridge of my nose, I took a long, calming breath. "Dalton, not liking someone isn't a reason to kill them. Besides, Kelly and Brandon were together when Sterling fell off the stage. She couldn't have been responsible for the accident."

Dalton narrowed his eyes. "Do you have any actual proof they were together?"

Darn it. He was right. All I had was Kelly's word, which wasn't good enough to clear her or Brandon.

"Okay, I'll give you that one, but we aren't going to figure this out tonight. I want to take a nice long bath and get in bed early, so you need to leave."

To my surprise, the ghost didn't argue. After I drew a bath and used one of the complimentary bath bombs, I dialed Jennifer's cell phone. She answered on the fifth ring, which was unusual for her.

"Oh, hi, April," she said, in an odd, staccato beat. "How's your trip going?"

"You sound out of breath. Is everything okay?" In the background I heard the kitchen door open, followed by a buzz of voices. "Who's there?"

"Just Irma's friends. Let me hand the phone to her."

Irma came on the line. "What do you want? I'm busy."

"You told me to call before I went to bed. What is going on in my house?"

Ignoring the question, she said, "It's only nine o'clock. What are you doing going to bed at this hour?"

"Because I've had a long day, complete with a flat tire on the way down here, and I'm fine. Thanks for asking."

A dismissive sound came over the line. "If you weren't fine, you'd have said so first. Have you caught the murderer?"

"Not yet." I wasn't about to give her an update until she answered my questions first. "Will you please tell me what's going on in my house?"

The response came out more guarded than I liked. "You said I could ask some friends over."

"Yes," I agreed, "but I didn't realize you meant a crowd."

"Who said anything about a crowd? They just talk a lot. When are you coming back?"

"Tomorrow. Probably late."

"Okay. See you then."

The line went dead. I held the handset out. "She hung up on me," I said in an astonished voice. "She actually hung up on me."

If I expected the device to answer me, it didn't. I started to worry about what was going on back in Serenity Cove, and then I shut down that internal voice. I was in a beautiful hotel room after a delicious dinner and a long soak in an antique tub. Tomorrow would be soon enough to deal with anything—murder or mayhem back at home.

Since Dalton didn't reappear that evening, I assumed he took my scolding about privacy to heart—until I woke up the next day to find him standing at the foot of my bed.

Sitting up and trying to focus my bleary eyes, I said, "Dalton, we talked about that."

"You're not naked," the ghost replied, as if that settled the whole business. "I was going to announce myself like you said, but you were still asleep, so I just stood here and waited until you woke up. Good morning."

"Good morning," I said, throwing back the covers and sitting on the edge of the bed trying to get my bearings.

The ghost was raring to go, even if I wasn't. "So," he said, clapping his hands. "What's the plan for the day?"

"You mean besides driving back to Serenity Cove?"

Dalton looked crestfallen. "You're not really leaving, are you? You told Violet you wouldn't go without seeing her first."

"I'm not going right away, but I would like to get home by early this evening."

"But what if you haven't figured out who murdered me by then?"

Running my hand through my hair, I said, "Let's see where we are after I talk to Kelly. I'm going to her shop after breakfast to see if her alibi for yesterday really does hold up. Now, go away so I can get dressed. I'm going to have breakfast downstairs, and I should be ready to leave in about an hour. Can you get to Kelly's on your own or do you need to meet me in the lobby?"

"I think I can get there," Dalton said. "I'm starting to get the hang of moving from one place to another, especially if I've been there before. I just close my eyes and picture the place and poof." He shut his eyes tightly.

"Okay, good. If you're not downstairs..." Before I finished my sentence, he'd disappeared. "Poof, indeed," I muttered.

After I dressed, I re-traced my steps to the elevator and found the same operator waiting for me. A few guests wandered around the lobby, but I had the restaurant mostly to myself, which allowed me to linger over two cups of fragrant Earl Grey while I enjoyed a short stack of buttermilk pancakes with blueberry compote and a side of crispy bacon.

Dalton hadn't shown up by the time I finished, so I assumed he would be waiting for me at Stockville Coffee Roasters.

The coffee shop was highlighted on the map of downtown I found in the lobby. The four-block walk got my blood pumping and gave me time to get my thoughts in order.

Of all the possible suspects, Violet still topped my list. She stood the most to gain from Dalton's death thanks to his life insurance policy, and she had no one to corroborate her whereabouts when Sterling tumbled off the stage.

Dalton had made it clear he didn't want to hear that theory, and I didn't much like the idea of Violet being a murderer either. It would be interesting to see what her best friend had to say about the possibility.

Given my occupation, I prefer tea over coffee most of the time, although Jennifer's morning creations had done a great deal to change that. But regardless, the rich aroma that enveloped me when I opened the door to Kelly's Coffee Roasters made my mouth water.

Like all the businesses in town, Kelly embraced an industrial, vaguely Steampunk vibe in decorating the shop. Whoever had the local wallpaper concession was raking in the dough, but rather than shooting for the genteel, opulent air both the theater and the hotel conveyed, Kelly had achieved something edgier.

From the fake gas lighting fixtures to the cabinets full of odd curiosities, the place could have been peeled from the pages of a Sherlock Holmes mystery. Period perfect, but with a fun twist that tickled the imagination and encouraged conversation.

Judging from the low drone of voices in the room, the décor had the desired effect. Kelly spotted me at the door and waved me over to the counter. In her own element, she seemed much more upbeat.

"It's nice of you to stop by." She offered me her hand. "Yesterday was trying."

"I'm glad I stopped in to see your business. This place is amazing."

"Thank you," she grinned, obviously pleased by the

complement. "What can I get for you? It's on the house."

"What would you suggest?"

"The special of the day is a honey vanilla latte."

"Then that's what I'll have. Will you join me?"

"Absolutely." Pointing, she said, "There's a table open in the back. Have a seat and I'll be right with you."

From the vantage point in the corner, I studied the crowd. Some patrons appeared to be students from the local community college, while other, more solitary souls sat tucked away in secluded nooks scribbling in their journals.

I loved the cheerful atmosphere of the tearoom, but it crossed my mind that the library Mark remodeled for me before he left town might be a nice place to serve coffee. When Kelly arrived with two generous, steaming mugs, I tucked that idea away for future consideration.

Telegraphing a mental apology to Jennifer and her barista skills, I said, "This is the best latte I've ever had."

"Thank you. We grind our own beans and I play around with blends. You looked like someone who would go for dark roast with a hint of sweetness."

Murder investigation or not, I laughed. "That's actually a pretty good description of me."

Dalton was nowhere in sight, but I didn't know how much time I had before he showed up, so I decided to dive right in. "How do you think Violet is coping with Dalton's death?"

"As well as can be expected. She found out yesterday morning that Dalton had a life insurance policy and she's the beneficiary. She wants to put all the money back into the theater because that's what Dalton would have wanted."

I feigned ignorance. "Is it a lot of money?"

"And then some. I told her she should at least put some money aside for the future-- maybe get herself a little house, but she wouldn't listen. Violet's too sweet and naïve for her own good, but maybe she'll come to her senses after the shock wears off. I've never seen her do one mean thing. Well, that's not true, there was one time, but that was years ago, and she was just a girl."

I wanted to hear the story, but as I feared, Dalton arrived, popping into the empty chair beside me. "Sorry. I got turned around and wound up at the library by mistake," the ghost said. "What did I miss?"

His sudden arrival startled me so much, I almost spilled my latte.

"I'm sorry," Kelly said, reaching out to steady my hand. "Is this conversation upsetting you?"

"No. I have a pinched nerve in my neck," I impro- vised. "It acts up when I'm under stress." I rubbed the back of my neck for good measure. "Dalton must have loved Violet a great deal to make her his insurance beneficiary."

"I know," Kelly said, looking uncomfortable. "I've been thinking about that. I always thought Dalton was too full of himself, but he was an actor. I mean, you met Edna." She chuckled. "It's a hazard of the profession. I didn't think he was right for Violet, but I may have judged him too harshly."

"That's not an unusual reaction," I said. "Often

when someone dies, we wish we'd treated them more fairly in life."

"I suppose that's true," she conceded. "I hate to see Violet suffering. She keeps saying how much she wishes she could bring Dalton back just long enough to tell him she loves him one more time."

A shadow fell over the table. We both looked up to see Brandon standing over us. "That sounds sweet enough, but it's the same line I'd use if I'd killed someone and wanted to make myself sound innocent."

The remark, coming out of nowhere, left us both at a loss for words until Kelly clicked her tongue and chided him. "Brandon, what a ridiculous thing to say. April will think you're serious." She turned toward me. "He's working on a murder mystery play to be performed at the theater. He never stops writing scenes in his head and sometimes they come out of his mouth."

"You're a playwright?" I asked.

Brandon shrugged. "I've written a few scripts." He turned to Kelly. "Would you see what's taking my order so long?"

Excusing herself, Kelly disappeared behind the counter. Brandon stood stiffly without speaking.

"Nice to see you again," I said hoping to ease the awkward moment.

"You keep popping up, *Aunt* April," he said in a bored voice. "Should I plan on seeing you everywhere I go?"

"I'm driving home this afternoon."

Kelly returned with two cardboard take-out trays filled with cups.

Brandon smiled, perhaps for Kelly's benefit. "It was good of you to come to the service. Your being there meant a lot to Violet."

He gave me a curt, dismissive nod and left.

CHAPTER 9

*K*elly rejoined me at the table, and I nodded toward the door. "Is he always wound that tight?"

Her expression was something between a smirk and a grimace. "Brandon doesn't process his emotions well. Dalton was his best friend and there's a lot riding on this production for Violet, and for the theater too. Brandon's working on getting touring companies to play Stockville. He's under a lot of pressure."

Probing gingerly at the topic, I said, "I've had the distinct feeling since we met that Brandon is suspicious of me for some reason."

She laughed. "It took me two years to get him to warm up to me. Don't take it personally. What do you do for a living, April?"

Even if the segue seemed abrupt, I couldn't see any harm in admitting I owned a tearoom. That revelation provided an instant bonding moment that resulted in a good hour of shop talk.

Kelly took me into the back to see the roasting equipment. After she explained all the steps of the process, she showed me the small selection of tea she kept on hand and asked what she could add to better serve her customers. I gave her advice on expanding the available choices, and she shared her thoughts on my idea to add a coffee room to the tearoom.

Even if I didn't learn any specific facts about Brandon, Violet, or the theater, I did develop an opinion about Kelly. After taking some time to get to know her, nothing about the woman's behavior made me suspicious of her in any way. If she and I lived in the same town, I thought we could easily be friends. I enjoyed the time we spent together and said so before I left.

"Me too," Kelly agreed. "I'm sorry we had to meet under such sad circumstances. Stop in if you're ever back in Stockville. Be safe on the road. No more flats."

"Thank you. I don't plan on any. The woman at the hotel told me where I can buy a new tire before I leave. Jackson's?"

"Jacobson's. It's on your left just before you hit the highway. You can't miss it. They're fast and affordable."

Both sounded good to me, but when I stepped onto the sidewalk, Dalton was lying in wait to pitch a fit about my plans. "You can't leave. You haven't solved my murder."

Glancing around to make sure no one was watching, I answered him as I started walking back toward the hotel.

"Yes, Dalton, I can leave and I'm going to leave as soon as I say goodbye to Violet. I think I've been pretty darn accommodating since you materialized in my kitchen uninvited. The only person I can see with a reason to kill you is Violet, and everyone—you included—says that's impossible."

"Of course, it's impossible. How can you even think such a thing after meeting her?"

"The fact that Violet wants to put all the insurance money right back into the theater means she has no motive. *If* she follows through on those plans, that is. But she seems genuinely distraught about your death, and I'm having trouble believing she'd harm a fly, much less commit murder."

"I told you—she's an angel. What about what your doctor friend said about the caffeine levels on my tox screen?"

"Maybe the stuff builds up in your system, I don't know." As I strolled along the sidewalk, I glanced into a cute café, checking out the décor. "My tearoom won't run itself."

"Your friends are taking care of that, and I thought you believed me."

"I believed there were enough questions surrounding your death to come down here and have a look around. And I did."

The ghost grimaced. "The murderer still needs to be caught and put behind bars. Violet told you she thinks she's in danger."

"And she retracted that and admitted she was just upset and being dramatic."

His jaw dropped open. "When did she say that?"

"At the reception after your funeral when she was

showing me around the theater." When he didn't answer, I added, "Fear and anxiety in her situation is normal. Her fiancé abruptly died. Her life is upside down. I'd be more concerned if she weren't upset and overwrought."

"What about the note Sterling got before he was shoved off the stage?"

I stopped in my tracks. That was one thing I couldn't explain away. Glancing at my watch and doing some mental math, I said, "Okay. Will it make you feel better if I talk with Sterling before I leave town?"

"Yes," the ghost said stubbornly, "because when you do, you'll see that you shouldn't be leaving town at all. Besides, Violet should be at the theater, and you promised to see her."

Perfect. Two birds, one stone.

"After we stop by the theater, I need to check out of the hotel, buy a new tire, and get home."

Getting that stubborn look again, Dalton said, "Doesn't that depend on what Sterling has to say?"

Now he was *really* starting to get on my nerves. "Just take the win, Dalton."

Giving me a grin and a shrug, the spirit floated along beside me as I walked past the hotel and down the street to the theater. I found the front door open and with help from Dalton, tracked Sterling down in his office backstage.

When I rapped lightly on the doorframe, the poor guy almost jumped out of his skin. "Oh!" he said. "It's you. Dalton's aunt, right?"

"Yes. I'm April. I wanted to come by before I left

town to see if you were okay after that tumble you took yesterday."

"That's nice of you, though not necessary," he said. "Let me find you a seat."

He hastily removed a box of programs from a folding chair beside his desk to make room for me.

From the doorway Dalton said, "Quit wasting time. Ask him about the note."

If he'd exercised two seconds of patience, that's where I was going next.

"I don't want to be nosy," I said, "but yesterday when I brought you that glass of water from the lobby, I thought I heard you tell Violet you'd found a threatening note on your desk."

For a fraction of a second the stage manager's eyes widened, but then he went into denial mode. "I don't know what you're talking about."

Despite my desire to spare Dalton's feelings, I pursued a different line of questioning. "You care a great deal about Violet, don't you?"

"Now wait just a minute!" Dalton yelped. "What's that supposed to mean?"

When the ghost spoke, the pens and pencils in a cup on Sterling's desk rattled and the room felt suddenly oppressive.

Sterling frowned. "Did you feel a tremor?"

"I'm not sure." I willed Dalton to calm down. "It might have just been the wind."

Cutting my eyes toward the door, I saw Dalton standing with his hands clenched into fists. I decided to risk him completely losing his cool. I needed to get an answer out of Sterling, and I could always run with the earthquake excuse if necessary.

"I was asking you about Violet?"

The stage manager looked down at his hands clasped loosely in his lap. He seemed helpless and downtrodden.

"Yes, I like Violet. She's a good friend."

The answer seemed to pacify Dalton because the air in the room grew lighter.

"You wouldn't want anything to happen to her, would you?" I prodded.

"Of course not," Sterling said, looking up with the earnestness of a schoolboy.

"Then tell me about the note. If someone threatened you, everyone in the theater company could be in danger, including Violet."

With deliberate care, he opened the middle desk drawer and brought out a sheet of copy paper, which he handed to me. I unfolded the note and read in block letters. *"Keep your mouth shut or else."*

"Keep your mouth shut about what?" I asked.

"I have no idea," Sterling replied, meeting my eyes directly. "If I did, I'd tell you. Really, yesterday was nothing. I probably just tripped."

"He's lying," Dalton said.

I got the feeling that rather than lying outright, Sterling was keeping something from me and everyone else. I wanted to ask him what he was hiding but thought better of it.

"Thank you for talking to me, Sterling." I stood to go. "Be more careful, okay?"

"You bet I will," he said, with a shy, grateful grin.

"By the way, is Violet here today?"

"No, I haven't seen her. Do you want me to ask her to call you?"

"I have her number. I'll call her before I drive back home."

Outside the doorway, Dalton hissed, "You're going home? Without solving my murder? You may be willing to leave Violet in danger, but I won't. I'll be by her side every minute."

Because Sterling was still within earshot, I couldn't answer, but I sent a silent prayer heavenward that Dalton wouldn't wind up an earthbound ghost like Chef. I'd done everything I could for the young actor. Now I needed to get back to my own life.

I returned to the auditorium and found the two theater ghosts on the stage.

"Oh, hey," Pearl called out to me. "You're back. We was just rehearsing."

I wanted to ask why, when they had no audience, but instead I asked, "What show are you doing?"

"Naughty Marietta. It was a big hit, and I was on my way to being a big star at the time of my unfortunate demise. Louis B. Mayer himself was gonna come see the show. He's a big-time movie producer, you know."

"I know." A long dead movie producer.

"We're practicing my big number, Ah, Sweet Mystery of Life. Wanna hear it?"

"Maybe another time." I made my way down the center aisle toward the exit.

"You don't know what you're missing." Pearl began

singing, and her soprano voice filled the auditorium. Louis B. would have been impressed, no doubt.

George appeared between us and the door. "Lady, did you find out who killed me?"

I gave Pearl a pointed look, and she took the hint. "You go on, I'll explain it to him. Again."

As I pushed the door to the lobby open, George called out to Dalton. "Hey, mister. You stay away from my dame, ya hear?"

Dalton stopped, then looked to me for an explanation.

I shrugged. "Just agree with him. Trust me, it's quicker."

"You got it, dude." He gave the other ghost a thumbs up. "I won't go near her."

"Glad to hear it, buddy."

Outside the theater, I tried Violet's number, but the call went to voice mail. *"Hi. This is Violet. I'll be away for a few days. Please leave a message and I'll get back to you."*

After the beep I said, "Hi, Violet. This is April. I'm glad you're taking some time for yourself. I'm so sorry to miss you, but I need to get back to Serenity Cove. I'll call you next week to see how you're doing. Thank you again for everything you did for Dalton."

Squaring my shoulders, I headed back to the Hotel Stockville. I didn't regret coming to town. The circumstances around Dalton's passing had seemed strange, but Sheriff Fontana was right. Not every death involved a murder.

Kelly was right on the money when she said the mechanics at Jacobson's garage were fast and affordable. An hour after I checked out of the hotel, I was on the road for Serenity Cove.

By the time I pulled into my driveway around five o'clock, I'd been largely successful in putting the events that had occurred in Stockville out of my mind. Cars lined the street along Ocean Drive, not an unusual sight on warm days when beachgoers parked from the lighthouse to the hotel, but today had been on the cool side and the sun would be setting soon. I guessed someone was having a party or barbecue.

The lights were on, but they looked different. I wondered if Jennifer had gotten one of those color wheels to change the lighting to blues and greens. She, along with Irma and Zoe would be tidying up after a busy Sunday. As I got out of the car and made my way around the back of the house, I decided to offer to order pizza from Tony's to thank them for manning the ship in my absence.

Then I opened the kitchen door and realized I'd been duped.

CHAPTER 10

*A*s I entered the kitchen through the back door, Jennifer entered from the front, giving me a view of the dining room. The undulating lights reminded me of Irma's defunct café.

I recognized some of the regulars from The Mermaid Café. Zoe stood at the sink washing dishes, while Irma stirred pots on the stove.

Everyone froze. Trying not to jump to any conclusions or lose my temper, I said, "Irma, what's going on here?"

Even knowing she'd been caught red-handed running a restaurant in my house when I'd already nixed the plan, Irma showed no sign of remorse. "You told me I could invite some people over for dinner." She turned down the flame on one of the burners. "So that's what I did."

Zoe shut off the tap, while Jennifer stood rooted in place in the doorway with a large serving tray balanced on the palm of her hand.

"Put that down before you drop it," I told her. "Are these people paying for their dinner?"

"A restaurant can't make money if people don't pay to eat," Irma informed me with infuriating calm. "Since you're here, we could use some help waiting tables."

Clenching my teeth, I said, "You have some nerve, you know that?"

Irma wasn't the kind of person to back down, but I thought I saw her flinch. We stood staring at one another until I broke the silence.

"I should tell all those people to leave, but I won't embarrass you like that. We'll talk about this tomorrow. I've had a really long couple of days, and I'm going upstairs. I'd prefer not to be bothered."

Halfway up the stairs, I heard the tap turn back on and the activity returned to normal, or what Irma considered normal anyway. For all the difference my arrival had made in their clandestine dining caper, I might as well have stayed in Stockville.

From the top of the stairs, I heard an inquisitive, "Meowrr?"

Whisk sat on the top stair silhouetted against the light in the upper hallway. When I passed the cat without speaking, he repeated the sound.

Glancing down, I said, "I've had a long day. Can we talk about this another time?"

The Bengal fell in beside me at a brisk trot, following me to the parlor door. "I guess that's a no." I sighed. "You want an answer right now?"

A rumbling purr answered my question.

I stopped and looked down into his glowing amber eyes. It felt as if we'd entered a kind of negotiation.

"You're trying to tell me that you want to live with Zoe."

The cat's head dipped in an imperceptible nod.

To my surprise, a knot came into my throat. I can't say that Whisk and I had ever gotten close, but I was used to the gorgeous creature's aloof presence in my life. And he was a surprisingly good listener. I'd miss having him to talk to.

"Okay. I'll ask her when all this blows over."

Cocking his head to the side, Whisk let out a concerned chirp.

"Don't worry. Zoe's not in trouble. She's just doing what her grandmother told her to do. But Irma *is* in trouble. Most *definitely* in trouble. But that won't affect your plans, I promise."

Satisfied, Whisk trotted back to the head of the stairs and stretched out with his head on his paws. If he couldn't go into the kitchen, he could at least get close enough to hear Zoe's voice. That was real love.

I realized I was still holding my bag. Backtracking, I deposited the luggage in my bedroom, and while I was there, changed into my pajamas.

Then I went to the parlor and did something completely out of the ordinary; I closed the door. When I said I didn't want to be bothered, I meant it. Not by anyone.

I didn't want to risk Jennifer coming to find me and catching the brunt of my anger toward Irma. I had no doubt the stubborn old woman had railroaded both young women into taking part in her covert restaurant scheme, which only made me angrier.

When Irma was their age and my house was a French restaurant, she'd worked here, so she knew exactly how to arrange the main room for maximum seating. Now I understood why all those cars were parked on the street out front.

Part of me wasn't surprised that Irma had engineered the deception, but another part felt betrayed. We'd had an adult conversation about why opening a restaurant together—even on a part-time basis— wouldn't work. My friend apparently told me what I wanted to hear and then did as she pleased.

Picking up the remote, I channel surfed until I landed on a cooking show where amateurs tried to recreate professionally baked desserts and cakes with complex decorations. Normally I laughed out loud at the epic and ludicrous failures, but the sounds drifting up from the first floor stoked my bad mood.

After about an hour, I heard car doors slamming on the street outside, and a while later, Jennifer's footsteps in the hall. She paused at the parlor door, but then continued to her bedroom. Wise decision.

I don't know when I fell asleep, but suddenly I found myself face to face with Edna Lovelace, who lectured me in her bad English accent. "Sometimes deviations from the script are necessary to make the play come to life. Lighten up, old girl."

Even though I knew the words were nothing more than a turn of phrase, I bristled, "I am not an old girl."

"And I'll never be an old boy," Dalton said, melting

through the doorway and into the parlor. "I'll be this age forever. You worried about your precious chef being stuck in that kitchen. Aren't you worried about me?"

Something that sounded like a gunshot echoed through the room. Swimming up through half consciousness, I opened my eyes enough to see Dalton standing by the television set. The light from the program landed on his top hat at an odd angle, making it look outrageously tall and thin.

"Are you really here?" I mumbled.

"Yes, I'm here. Violet is in danger. Do something."

Not sure if I was performing the actions or dreaming them, I turned off the television and stumbled to my bedroom. I fell fast asleep, but instead of a restful night, I ran around backstage at the Elliott Theater in my dreams, trying to hand out props.

Laughter from the audience made me look onstage and there lay Dalton, dead on the boards with the other actors stepping over him. At my elbow, Edna said gaily, "The show must go on, and you're not in it."

One of those cheesy, oversized vaudeville canes they used to jerk lousy performers off the stage shot out of the darkness, snagged me around the waist, and started jerking me into a pit filled with cats guzzling energy drinks.

Gasping, I sat up in bed, feeling frantically in the bedclothes for the cane's restraining hook. Sunlight streamed through the windows and the house was completely quiet.

For a brief minute, I panicked about opening the

tearoom on time, but then remembered it was Monday. We were closed, and I could go down in my robe and slippers to get a badly needed cup of coffee.

Going by the clock on the bedside table, Jennifer had already left for class, which was just as well. I couldn't promise anyone that I'd be in a good mood today. I wasn't sure if Dalton had really appeared to me the night before, but all the wild, jumbled imagery in my dreams certainly resulted from my trip to Stockville—not to mention my irritation over Irma's stunt.

The thing was, I didn't care all that much that she served dinner to a pack of her regulars. What bothered me was that she lied to me. If I knew Irma, she'd make me track her down to have our inevitable confrontation, but I wanted and deserved an explanation—and an apology.

My mind churned with all the things I wanted to say to her, so much so that I gasped and almost tripped over my own feet when I found Dalton standing in the middle of the kitchen waiting.

"Don't do *that!*" I barked.

"Do what?" he asked, his shoulders drooping. "I was just waiting for you, respecting your privacy like you asked."

"I'm sorry—you just startled me. I had a rough night." I considered telling him about my dream, but it had nearly faded away. "Why aren't you in Stockville? The last time I saw you, you swore you'd never leave Violet's side again."

"I can't find her, April. Please. You've got to help me."

"Slow down. Tell me exactly what happened."

According to Dalton, after I left Stockville, he went back inside the theater. In Violet's dressing room, he found a sheet of paper lying unfolded on the vanity. The message, also in block letters like Sterling's note, read, "You're next."

I had to admit that sounded ominous, especially considering Sterling had been pushed off the stage after receiving a similar note. But "you're next," could mean anything. For all we knew, it wasn't even connected to the murder.

"Dalton, I'm sure Violet just needs some alone time to grieve your death. I don't really understand how these things work, but it's possible you can't find her because she's shielding herself from you."

Behind me the spices in the rack rattled and a measuring spoon hanging on a hook fell into the sink with a clatter.

"Okay, calm down," I said, holding out my hand. "Losing your temper won't help."

"I don't want to lose my temper," the ghost said through gritted teeth. He glanced over at the spice rack and his eyes widened. "Did I make that happen?"

I nodded. "It seems that when you get upset or angry, things start moving. Maybe you send out a vibrational field. I'm not sure how it works—most ghosts can't move things, at least the ghosts I've met." I'd only met a few, and I planned to keep it that way.

His eyebrows knitted together. "I want to be able to do it on purpose."

Understanding his frustration, I tried again. "I'm sure there are all kinds of things you want to do, including finding Violet. If you aren't going to move on, Dalton, you'll need to learn to control your emotions or something bad could happen."

Dalton didn't appear to listen to me. "I'm headed back to Stockville. Something is wrong, and Violet is in danger. I don't know how to make you see that, but it's true. I know it's true."

Instead of disappearing, the ghost walked to the back door and reached for the knob to open it. He grasped the handle but couldn't turn it. Instead, his frustration got the better of him and he shook the knob. His vibrations moved the air and a few items fell off the pantry shelves.

Dalton gave up trying to open the door, instead walking through it like a normal ghost. I worried he wouldn't be a happy haunt so long as questions lingered about his death, but what more could I do about it?

CHAPTER 11

*A*s much as I enjoyed having Jennifer around the house and working with her in the kitchen, I was happy to have some well-needed time alone. A quick check of the supplies on hand told me we had plenty of finger sandwich fillings for the next day, but I was low on shepherd's pies, quiches, and pastries.

When my stomach grumbled, I resolved to make the first batch of fruit and cream cheese breakfast pastries for myself. I retrieved the puff pastry sheets from the refrigerator and lightly rolled them out, then cut four circles. I placed the circles on the baking sheet and after scoring a circle around the edge, I added a sweetened cream cheese mixture and topped them with fresh blueberries in the center. The scoring allowed the outside of the pastries to rise, making a border around the cream cheese and fruit.

Since the recipe was one of the simplest in my repertoire, it took no time for a sheet of pastries to go in the oven. While they baked, I made a pot of coffee with the traditional, manageable coffee percolator that had come with the house and still worked perfectly.

By the time the pastries were ready to come out of the oven, I had a steaming cup of dark roast at the ready. Sliding the hot pastries onto a dish, I dove into what proved to be a remarkably self-indulgent morning meal.

On the third pastry, I slowed down enough to open the drawer in the island where I kept my notepads and pencils. Eyeing pastry number four, I started to doodle on the paper, sketching out the facts of Dalton's murder as I knew them.

No matter how many words I circled or arrows I drew connecting one circumstance to another, all roads led back to Violet. But I didn't believe she was a murderer any more than Dalton did. My gut told me Violet wouldn't have the nerve to kill someone, much less the cold calculation to carry out such a plan.

In my head I saw the girl's large luminous eyes, red-rimmed from crying over Dalton. The black shadow I imagined looming behind her looked a heck of a lot like Brandon. What if I was wrong? What if Violet really was in danger? Nothing about Brandon's behavior at the theater said, "grieving best friend." In fact, he'd glared at me every time I mentioned Dalton.

My cell phone, which I'd tossed on the island when I came downstairs, buzzed. I saw Irma's name on the screen. For the most part, I wasn't a coward, but by no stretch of the imagination was I ready to have it out with my friend. I let the call go to voice mail and then listened to the recording.

"Look, I get that you're mad. But we're going to have to talk sooner or later because I'm getting tons of calls asking to make reservations for next Saturday night. If you'd quit being so stubborn, you'd see that we have a gold mine on our hands. We raked in the dough last night. By the way, we need to order some nice steaks."

Under my breath, I muttered. *"I'm* stubborn? Talk about the pot calling the kettle black."

I didn't feel ready to talk on the phone, so I typed out a text. *"I think you missed the point. As usual."* I deleted that last part, instead adding, *"You lied to me."*

After I hit send, I did my best to put Irma and her shenanigans out of my mind. I needed a distraction, and I had just the thing—whatever was or wasn't going on in Stockville.

"Dalton?" I called out. "Can you stop by? If you're not too busy?" Why a ghost would be busy, I didn't know, but it seemed the polite thing to say. "Let's talk some more about Violet."

No answer.

I poured myself a second cup of coffee and stared at my notes, doodles, and arrows. My intuition told me Dalton and I needed to make sure Violet was safe. Dalton couldn't do much, but I could do something. But what?

"Dalton?" I called out again.

Huh. Chef usually answered me when I called out to him, but he never left the house. I realized I didn't know how to talk with a ghost at a distance, much less summon one to appear. But maybe if I was in Stockville, Dalton would be able to hear me.

The phone buzzed and Irma's name flashed on the display, but I ignored it. This time I didn't listen to the message, instead sending a text to Jennifer. *Going out. Be back late. Don't wait up.*

After a few seconds, her message appeared: *Sorry about last night.*

Not your fault, I wrote, adding a smiling emoji hoping she understood I wasn't mad at her. After some time away from my friends, maybe I'd be ready to talk.

Gulping down the last of my coffee, I double checked that the oven was off before wrapping up the last pastry and putting it in the refrigerator. I set my cup and plate in the sink and ran upstairs to change.

In less than an hour, I was on my way back to Stockville. I already knew where I'd go first—Kelly's coffee shop. I felt certain Kelly had more information about the inner workings of the Revival Theater Group. Also, from what she'd told me before, she'd known Violet since she was a girl and might have some insights into her character. I didn't expect her to tell me if she thought Violet capable of murder, but she might let something slip.

She also knew Brandon well, I assumed, and I hadn't crossed him off my suspect list. Far from it, since his possessiveness toward Violet made me wonder if he was in love with her. Had his feelings for her led him to kill his supposed best friend?

I'd been giving some thought to Freddie's reaction to

the amount of caffeine in Dalton's system when he died. Kelly ran a coffee shop—did that give her access to large amounts of purified caffeine? I hadn't gotten a lethal vibe off her during our conversation the day before, but it wouldn't be the first time I'd misjudged a murderer.

On this trip, the highway gods smiled on me. I made the drive without car trouble or getting a ticket, stopping at a roadside coffee shop along the way to grab a sandwich when the pastries wore off.

My watch read a quarter to one when I parked in front of Coffee Roasters and cut the engine. Taking a few moments to pull my thoughts together and decide what to say without rousing suspicions, I took a deep breath and got out of the car. Kelly spotted me the instant I stepped inside.

Weaving her way through the crowded tables, she gave me a warm smile. "April! I thought you went back to Serenity Cove yesterday."

"I did, but I could hardly sleep last night because I left without seeing Violet after promising I would. I've tried to call her several times and she hasn't answered, so I came back."

Kelly's eyebrows went up. "Sounds like you're worried about her. Why?"

Not wanting to tell her the inside information I had thanks to Dalton, I merely nodded. "Do you know where I can find Violet?"

Casting a furtive glance at the patrons filling the tables by the windows, she gestured to the back of the room. "The table where we sat before is open. Have a seat, and I'll get us something to drink. How does a latte sound?"

"Sounds like a great pick-me-up after the long drive."

Minutes later, we were seated across from one another over steaming cups. Kelly leaned closer, keeping her voice low. "I don't want to add to your worries, but Violet received a threatening note like the one Sterling found on his desk. It scared her so much that she's gone into hiding until we're sure she's safe. I promised I wouldn't tell anyone where she is, but she's safe."

Considering the amount of strain Violet had been under since Dalton's death, I could understand the poor girl feeling the need to go into hiding, but not with a huge career opportunity looming on her horizon.

"What did the note say?" I already knew, but I wanted to hear it from her.

"It said, 'you're next.'"

"What does that mean?" I asked. "Next for what?"

"That's the thing," she admitted. "We don't know. Maybe it's from the same person who pushed Sterling off the stage."

"That makes sense, I suppose." Probably the same person who gave Dalton the overdose of caffeine.

"I'm sure it's just a prank," Kelly said, though the worry lines between her eyebrows told me differently. "But she's been through a lot lately, so we both figured a little getaway couldn't hurt."

Trying to get a read on the depth of Kelly's ambitions, I asked, "But what about the play?"

"As her understudy, I'm taking over the role until Violet feels safe to come back."

A perfectly reasonable and ostensibly caring answer, but a tad too pat for my tastes. I didn't know that much about the theater world, but I suspected every understudy felt the temptation of wishing the lead would miss at least one performance. But if that was Kelly's motive, how did Dalton's death fit into her plans?

"Isn't the agent Brandon contacted coming down to see the production this weekend?"

I couldn't be certain, but I thought I detected a flicker of annoyance in Kelly's eyes.

"He's a producer—quite influential in Hollywood. It was a real coup to get him to agree to come to one of our performances. No one wants Violet to miss his visit," she assured me, "especially not me. But her safety and peace of mind are the most important things."

"Absolutely," I murmured, buying myself time to think by sipping my latte. That gave me an idea to find out more about Kelly's background. "Your drinks are so good; you must have been doing this for ages."

The flattery had the desired effect. "Thanks, but actually, I've only been running Coffee Roasters for a couple of years."

"What did you do before that?"

"I lived in L.A. and tried to make a career for myself in acting."

Interesting, and potentially incriminating. "Really? Have I seen you in anything?"

She rattled off an impressive series of small roles—the stewardess in a film about a hijacking, the secretary to a lawyer kidnapped in a spy movie that came out ten years earlier, and a number of commercials for everything from dish liquid to car batteries.

"It sounds like you had a great deal of work," I said. "Why did you stop and move to Stockville of all places?"

A pained expression came over her face. "You're right, I landed a decent number of roles, but I never got my big break. As I got older, the jobs were fewer and farther between, and I had to accept that I needed to do something else with my life. Violet is just getting started and the perfect age for a producer to come along and discover her. She has a sort of charisma that attracts attention, something I suppose I never had."

"But you're still acting." I felt bad that she seemed to feel her best years were past her. "Why just an understudy role?"

She chuckled. "It's just for fun now. But one thing I'll say about my acting career—it paid for this coffee shop. When I saw a listing for this place online, I drove up from L.A. to look at the property. Violet came with me and met Dalton the same day. A few weeks later, we both moved to Stockville, and the rest is history."

"It seems to have worked out well for you," I said, nodding toward the crowded tables, "but what a shame for Violet to miss this big break if she's such a good actress."

"Oh, no," Kelly said, quickly correcting me. "I didn't say she was good. She has presence. People remember her, but in terms of acting, as much as I hate to say this about my dearest friend, Violet gets by on charm and personality."

Her words seemed completely at odds with how she claimed to feel about Violet. Who would tell a near stranger like me that their close friend had no talent. Was Kelly hiding bone-deep disappointment over her thwarted career ambitions?

She must have noticed my surprise, because she added, "I know that seems harsh, but what Violet lacks she can gain through experience and classes that will allow her to take her acting to the next level. I want that for her more than anything. The last thing I want to do is take Violet's chance away, especially since I have no illusions that any producer is going to be interested in me. Not at my age."

She had to be a decade younger than me. "At your age? You can't be more than, what? Late thirties?"

"I'm thirty-eight. Still young for almost anything other than Hollywood." Her regret was palpable. "Sorry, I didn't mean to go on and on about myself. Would you like me to get a message to Violet?"

"Yes, please. Tell her I'm back in town for the afternoon and I really want to see her. I'll go anywhere she likes and take any precautions that will make her feel safe."

"It may take a while before she gets back to me. She's notoriously slow responding to texts, but she'll text back eventually. Where are you planning to go next? Doing some sightseeing?" She chuckled. "There's not a lot to see in our little town."

Was Kelly trying to get rid of me? I brushed the idea aside realizing she most likely had to get back to work.

Reaching for a napkin, I wrote down my cell number. "I intended to donate to the theater fund in Dalton's memory before I left yesterday, but what with the tire repair, I forgot. I think I'll go over to the Elliott Theater, drop off a check, and maybe spend some time in Dalton's dressing room. For some reason, I feel close to him there."

Kelly responded with sympathy. "Of course. That's perfectly understandable. I'll call you as soon as I've heard from Violet."

After finishing my drink, I waved goodbye to Kelly and stepped outside into the bright sunshine.

I'd expected my ghost to meet me at the coffee shop, but there was no sign of him. "Where are you, Dalton?"

CHAPTER 12

his time when I climbed the front steps of the Elliott Theater, I found the double doors locked. The front windows were dark and when I put my ear against the wood, I couldn't hear any sounds from inside.

Returning to the sidewalk, I weighed my options. On the right side, the building backed up to a vacant lot with no access road, but on the left an alley led toward the back of the building. The gravel showed signs of traffic, which told me the stage entrance must be at the rear of the theater.

Sure enough, I found a green utility door. The parking spaces were empty, making me think no one would be in the theater, but when I turned the knob, the door opened.

I stepped into the cavernous darkness of backstage and stood blinking until my eyes adjusted. The building felt chilly and re-defined the concept of creepy.

The only illumination came from the single ghost light on the stage. Making my way slowly in the near darkness, I found myself outside Violet's dressing room. The door was ajar. Screwing up my courage, I pushed it open only to find a distraught Dalton pacing the small space in frenzied circles.

Spotting me, he let out a pitiful cry. "I can't find her anywhere. I've tried and tried..." He collapsed into a chair, his head in his hands. "I close my eyes and think of her, but when I open them, I'm still here."

"Calm down," I soothed. "I'm sure Violet is fine. She's gone into hiding just to be safe."

The ghost stopped. Even though he no longer needed to breathe, his chest heaved with emotion. "Hiding? Why? What happened?"

"You saw the note, remember? I think it really scared her." As I went through the scant details Kelly shared with me, Dalton's pale face took on the hue of a nice rosé. In life, I suspected his skin would have been crimson with emotion. From my limited experience, it seemed the dead who lingered on this plane carried a lot of life habits with them to the other side.

Chef had often worked on a new cookbook in a notebook that only he could see. Or he stood at the stove and stirred a pot of coq au vin that wasn't really there. Dalton was an actor accustomed to using his body to illustrate emotions. I'd never seen him on stage, but he pulled off agitation brilliantly.

When I finished speaking, the spirit all but shouted at me. "Hiding doesn't mean Violet is safe."

Trying not to feed into his growing alarm, I said, "It

also doesn't mean she's in danger. Give Violet credit for knowing what she needs, Dalton. She's probably completely overwhelmed and craving peace and quiet."

"Stop placating me," he snapped.

"I'm not placating you. I'd be more worried about Violet if she hadn't gone away."

He paced the small room while he thought over my words, then turned to me. "Kelly could have written the note to get Violet out of the way to resurrect her acting career."

"You think Kelly would have done that to her best friend?"

He scowled. "Some people will do almost anything when they feel desperate."

"Kelly didn't seem at all desperate to me. She assured me that Violet is safe, and I'm inclined to believe her."

Dalton stomped his foot with enough force to rattle the make-up bottles on the dressing table. "She's not safe! I can sense it. Something isn't right and while we're standing here arguing, Violet is in danger. Were you at least able to find out where Violet is? I need to see for myself that she's okay."

"Kelly wouldn't tell me, but maybe Violet's staying at her place." That was a reasonable assumption and one that should be easy enough for a ghost to investigate. Dalton needed something to do other than haunt an empty theater. "Why don't you pop over to Kelly's house?"

Dalton appeared ready to burst into tears. "I don't know where Kelly lives. She used to have an apartment over the coffee shop, but she moved into a bigger place a month or two ago. Violet was going to take me over to see the house, but I died before we could go."

"What's all the commotion?" Pearl had appeared, her hands on her hips. "There's enough racket to raise the dead." She chuckled. "Raise the dead, get it?" She spotted Dalton. "Hey sugar, what's your name?"

Dalton turned to me for support, but when I shrugged, he said, "I'm Dalton."

"Well, ain't you cute."

At that, George appeared. I whispered to Dalton, "Let's get out of here while we can."

Behind me a man's voice asked, "Who are you talking to?"

Snapping my head to look behind me, I found the stage manager, Sterling, standing in the doorway. He didn't look the least bit pleased to see me back in Stockville.

"Hi, Sterling," I said, laying a hand over my hammering heart. "You almost scared me to death. I didn't think anyone was here."

He narrowed his eyes. "Is someone with you?"

"No, no one at all. I have a habit of talking to myself. To be honest, I was talking to Dalton, not that he can hear me of course, but I feel close to him in this theater. It's almost like I can feel his presence."

Dalton chuckled. "That's an understatement."

The stage manager didn't look as if he bought one word of my excuse. "I had an errand to run. I guess I forgot to lock the door."

Trying to sound contrite, I said, "Sorry. My real

reason for coming back was to see Violet. I promised I'd see her before I went home, and I felt bad for breaking the promise. Have you seen her?"

Shoving his hands in his pockets, he said, "She's taking some time off, is what I heard. Not sure when she's coming back."

Did Sterling believe his own words or was he hiding something? Either way, Dalton was about to blow a fuse. If he let out a real burst of energy, who knew what might happen in the dressing room.

"Sterling, I talked to Kelly. I know Violet received a threatening letter, too."

The guy looked like a kid who'd been caught with his hand in a cookie jar. "Kelly probably shouldn't have told you that."

"So, you knew about the note?"

"Violet showed it to me and asked for my advice. I told her she was perfectly safe, that I could keep an eye on her to make sure nothing bad happened. If you ask me, it's a prank someone is having at our expense."

"Who would do such a thing?" I asked. "And don't forget, someone pushed you off the stage."

He scowled. "I don't want to accuse anyone without having any real evidence."

Beside me, Dalton said, "He's not telling you everything he knows."

No kidding.

Treading carefully, I said, "Do you know anything about Dalton's death that you haven't shared with me or the others? If you do, it might have some bearing on who threatened you and now Violet."

His eyes widened. "Me? Why would I know anything?"

"Well, you're the stage manager. It's your business to know what goes on in the theater, isn't it?"

Sterling's lips tightened into a thin line. He crossed his arms in a defensive posture. "If you want to ask me about the play, or the props, or how the lights work, I can tell you, but how would I know who's putting notes in people's dressing rooms?"

"What about Dalton's death?" I asked. "Do you know anything about that?"

His jaw clenched and his face reddened. "His death was an accident, everyone knows that. It was his own fault, chugging down all those energy drinks." He stopped talking and took a few deep breaths to calm himself. When he spoke again, he sounded more curious than angry. "What makes you think any different?"

His change in attitude wasn't lost on me. Was he trying to find out how much I knew?

"There are a lot of unanswered questions about my nephew's death and the notes that you and Violet received, that's all," I said noncommittally. "All I want right now is to see Violet, so I could see for myself that she's okay."

Sterling's features softened. "I'm worried about her, too."

In the distance, a phone rang. "That's the landline in my office," he said. "Hang on. I'll be right back."

As he exited, Dalton said, "You're not buying any of this, are you?"

"Hush and let me think."

Maybe I *was* being too easy on Kelly. If she wrote the notes to Sterling and Violet, she could be the killer. But why would she want Dalton dead? Disliking him or thinking he wasn't good enough for Violet wasn't enough motive in my book. But then, I've never wanted to kill anyone.

For the moment, however, the why of the murder didn't matter. If Violet was in danger, we needed to find out where she was staying. The obvious choice was her best friend's house, which meant we needed to find out where Kelly lived.

I was right in the middle of telling Dalton that when my phone rang. I ignored the call, but then I heard the ping signaling a text message. Fishing the device out of my pocket, my eye went straight to the word, "EMERGENCY."

The text was from Jennifer. Scanning the lines, I let out an uncharacteristic burst of profanity. My nemesis, Mayor Wanda Gasden, had gotten wind of Irma's dinner "party" and showed up at the tearoom, pitching a fit about permits.

When Jennifer told her I was out of town, the mayor pasted a notice on the door declaring the business to be in violation of code and closed us down until further notice. We were closed on Mondays anyway, but I needed to straighten things out before we opened tomorrow.

"On my way," I thumb-typed. "And tell Irma she better be there waiting for me when I get back."

Before I left the theater, I stuck my head into Sterling's office. He put his hand over the receiver and gave me a quizzical look. "I have to get home and deal with an emergency, but I'll be back to see Violet. Please tell her if you see her."

Speaking into the receiver, he said, "Let me call you back." Replacing the handset in the cradle, he stood. "I will if I see her. Let me show you out."

"That's really not necessary."

"Please. I insist. Follow me."

As we moved through the darkened auditorium, Dalton pleaded with me non-stop to stay in Stockville, but I couldn't answer him until Sterling let me out the front door. It may have been my imagination, but the stage manager seemed to turn the lock behind me with pointed emphasis.

"Nice to see you again, too," I muttered under my breath as I started down the steps.

"You can't do this," Dalton said. "Can't you see Sterling is acting weird?"

"A lot of people are acting weird, Dalton." I walked around the front to my car. "I've found that happens when you start asking probing questions about someone who's died. People aren't comfortable talking about death, and they're even less comfortable talking about murder."

"We need to find out what's really going on around here," Dalton insisted as he hurried alongside me. "We need to find out the truth."

I wanted to get to the truth too, but Irma's restaurant stunt had me between a rock and a code violation.

"Dalton, please try to understand. I care about you

and Violet, but there's a serious problem with my business. The tearoom means as much to me as this theater means to you. I wouldn't leave if I thought Violet was in real danger."

"That's reassuring." His sarcastic tone was impossible to miss.

I ignored his comment. "Try to find out as much information as you can on your own and come get me if you find Violet or learn anything important. Can you do that?"

The spirit nodded weakly. "Promise you'll come back?"

"I promise."

As I pulled away, I looked in the rear-view mirror and saw Dalton standing on the sidewalk, a faint outline against the gray concrete. I would come back, but first I had to clean up Irma's mess.

CHAPTER 13

*A*ll the way home, my mind jerked back and forth like a metronome. On one beat I weighed the possible clues in Dalton's death, and on the other rehearsed what I planned to say to Irma. The sun hung low over the horizon when I parked in front of the tearoom and marched up the steps.

A threatening pink notice decorated the center of my front door. It ripped neatly in two when I yanked if off the wood, taking some of the paint with it.

"Stupid Mayor," I groused.

I wadded the offending paper into a tight ball, which I shoved into my pocket. Then, taking a deep breath, I turned the knob and went inside. All the perpetrators sat waiting for me around a roaring fire: Jennifer, Irma, Zoe with Whisk in her arms—and Freddie.

"What are you doing here?" I asked Freddie. "There aren't any bodies for you to examine—yet." I sent an angry glare in Irma's direction. She glared back defiantly.

"Now, now," Freddie soothed. "Let's not go there."

My suspicious side flared. "Wait a minute. You didn't have anything to do with this fiasco, did you?"

"I did not," Freddie said firmly. "And I may even have told the principal culprit that she never should have tried to keep secrets from you."

An irritated *harrumph* came out of Irma's mouth.

Freddie ignored Irma. "Jennifer called me to play referee because she knew this would be a difficult conversation."

"I don't need a referee," I said in a tight voice. "I need an apology from my friend who lied to me, and then I need a strategy to get the mayor off my back."

The word "lied" hit Irma hard. To her credit, she looked properly guilty, even if she wasn't ready to back down. "I didn't mean to lie to you. I wanted to show you that the restaurant idea would work."

Our eyes locked. On the other side of all that obstinance, I saw a glimmer of hurt, which was the one thing Irma and I seemed to have in common. We both had a strong façade we used to cover our inner vulnerability. That realization softened me.

"Whether you meant to or not," I said, "you lied to me, and it hurt. And I acknowledge that my refusal to listen to your ideas for us to work together may have hurt you, too."

Freddie laid her hand on my arm. "That's a good place to start. Come on. Sit down. We'll talk this thing through and figure out what to do. Together. Like friends, because that's what we all are."

A lump rose in my throat so I couldn't speak. Instead, I nodded and plopped on the couch next to Zoe. Whisk instantly extricated himself from her embrace and settled in my lap, something he rarely did. As my hand fell on the cat's silky coat, I said in a choked voice, "You're not supposed to be in here."

"We didn't think it would matter this time because the mayor already shut you down," Zoe said. "I'm so sorry, April. We didn't mean to cause so much trouble."

Irma cleared her throat. "There's only one trouble-maker here. Me. I shouldn't have…" She seemed to have trouble getting the word out. She tried again. "I shouldn't have lied to you, and I'm sorry. And I should have checked your permits. Mayor Wanda Gasden has been after you ever since you torpedoed her plans to turn the library into a food court. Most of all, I should have respected your wishes when you said you didn't want me to run my restaurant out of your tearoom."

Infuriating though she was, Irma always did the right thing in the end. Swallowing around the lump in my throat, I said, "I wasn't against your restaurant idea. I was just afraid if we tried to work together it might hurt our friendship. I thought you understood that."

"I didn't," Irma admitted, "and I'm stubborn. I'll call my regulars and tell them next Saturday is off. Are we good?"

"We're good," I said, and then curiosity got the better of me. "How much money did you clear last night?"

She quoted a figure that represented a week's profit for the tearoom. I had to fight not to let my jaw drop. "You're kidding."

She puffed up in pride. "If there's one thing I know how to do, it's sling hash."

I didn't care about the money since the tearoom provided me with a comfortable living. What I did care about was Irma, and she'd been in a funk ever since her café had been destroyed.

I might as well give into the inevitable. "I suppose if the kitchen isn't big enough for the both of us, I could always go to another room."

Irma grinned. "Do you mean it? But what about the permits?"

"There's nothing wrong with my permits," I said. "I don't know what…" Then it hit me. "You didn't serve cocktails, did you?"

"Just Scotch and bourbon," Irma replied. "Your liquor cabinet needs work."

I felt irritation creep up my spine and had to force myself to keep my voice calm. "I don't have a liquor license. I'm only allowed to serve beer and wine."

A chorus of groans circled the room. I couldn't be sure, but I think Whisk even joined in.

"Okay," Freddie said. "Apology done; problem identified. Now, what do we do about this situation?"

Remembering the wad of paper in my pocket, I pulled out the notice, smoothed the two pieces flat, and arranged them on my lap. There was a handwritten note at the bottom.

"*Ms. May, I spotted a feline in your tearoom, which is a*

violation of the health code. The inspector will be paying a call on your premises. If he finds so much as one cat hair, you're done. — W. Gasden."

Well, that sealed the adoption deal. "Zoe, Whisk and I have talked, and he'd like me to ask you something."

"Yes?" Zoe waited expectantly.

"He'd like to come live with you. How does that sound?"

"O-M-G, really?!" she squealed, looking over at her grandmother. "Is it okay with you?"

"Well," Irma said gruffly, "I really don't have much choice now, do I?"

Zoe broke into happy tears and jumped to her feet. "Can Jennifer and I go buy some things for him? I mean, if we're done here."

"Go," I said, making a shooing motion with my hand. "We'll come up with a way to deal with the health inspector tomorrow. Go on, Whisk. Go with Zoe."

The Bengal turned his lovely gold eyes toward me and blinked slowly. He sat up and rested his front paws on my chest, touching his nose lightly to mine. That did it. Tears rolled down my cheeks. "Am I allowed to give you a hug?"

When the cat nestled closer, I cradled Whisk in my arms. "I'll miss you, you little rascal. Take good care of Zoe for me."

Whisk let me hand him over to his new mom, who held him tenderly and protectively. "We'll take care of each other, I promise. And I'll bring him back to visit, but only outside. Thank you so, *so* much, April."

"Take his carrier," I said. "He won't go inside for me, but I bet he will for you."

As predicted, Whisk walked in the open door of his bright pink crate without a meow of protest, tucking his tail against his body at the last minute.

Jennifer went along at Zoe's request to make sure they picked out items that would please Whisk's refined tastes. Irma held the door open to let the girls and her new grand-cat pass through.

Before she left, my crotchety friend gave me a lopsided grin. "You're thinking about those profits, aren't you?"

"Don't push it," I warned her with a smile. "We'll discuss that after we deal with the mayor."

Giving me a mock salute, she exited and closed the door. I looked over at Freddie. "Want to raid the refrigerator with me?"

"Sure." She followed me into the kitchen. "Where were you today, anyway?"

"I went back to Stockville." While I reheated leftovers from Irma's cooking spree, I caught Freddie up on the case.

"Wow," she said. "A lot has happened since we spoke on the phone."

"My money's on Kelly, the coffee lady, since she'd have access to the murder weapon. Still, it seems there'd be easier ways to get a chance to perform in front of a producer. And why kill Dalton? Violet is the only person who had a good motive to kill him because of the insurance, but there is no way that girl is a murderer. Although..." A million dollars was a lot of money.

"Although what?"

I shook my head. "Nothing."

"You're all over the place with your theories." Freddie watched me prepare a plate for each of us. "You know, caffeine in powder or pill form is easy to get ahold of. You don't need to own a coffee shop."

I sat down with my dinner. "I hadn't thought of that. I still don't see that any of these people have a motive for murder."

"From what I've learned, almost anyone can commit murder under the right circumstances. You wanted to throttle Irma when you walked in the front door tonight."

"That's for sure." I got back up and uncorked a bottle of red wine, pouring each of us a glass. "I didn't think I'd ever forgive her and now I'm considering sharing my kitchen with her. She's miserable not having a restaurant to run and people to feed."

"You'd be doing a community service," Freddie agreed, chewing happily. "If I have to eat one more taco, I'll explode like a piñata." When I didn't respond, "Tacos, piñata... get it?"

"Sorry. I'm still thinking about a motive for Dalton's murder. His best friend Brandon, the director, has conveniently moved into Dalton's role, not just in the play, but as Violet's protector. What if he'd fallen in love with Violet and decided to get rid of the competition?"

Freddie shook her head. "I hope that's not true. Talk about the ultimate betrayal."

"But if it is true, we owe it to Violet to make sure that Brandon doesn't end up as her new boyfriend. She's vulnerable right now, and…" I stopped talking as a thought came into my mind. "What if Violet is staying with Brandon?"

"If he *is* in love with her, then that might be the safest place for her to be right now," Freddie mused. "And if he's after her money, she's safe at least until she gets the check from the insurance company."

"But what if it's not about the money?" I asked.

Freddie speared a thick piece of pot roast. "The best way to protect Violet is to solve the murder. The best way would be to find out who put the caffeine in Dalton's drink. But once you solve that mystery, how are you planning to prove it?"

"I have no idea." I sighed, thinking of the lack of reliable clues. "I don't suppose we could find out if Brandon bought a whole bunch of caffeine pills?"

Freddie shook her head. "They're available over the counter as diet pills or to help keep you alert."

"That's not helpful."

Freddie declined my invitation to stay for dessert. "I have to go back to the office and work on some autopsy notes or the DA will have my head on a platter," she said. "We'll talk tomorrow. Get some sleep, okay? You look exhausted."

We hugged and I walked her out, waving from the front porch as she got into her car. The warm evening breeze and the rhythmic sound of the waves soothed me, so I made a cup of chamomile tea and carried it back out to the porch. I found myself mesmerized by the rolling waves across the street.

Dalton materialized in the chair next to me. I must have been getting used to him, because I wasn't startled when I realized I had company.

"Hi." I glanced at the forlorn-looking ghost. "Did you find Violet?"

"No," the ghost said mournfully. "I don't know anything more than I did when you left. What if something has happened to her?"

Maybe it was the dreamy quality of the evening or the soothing chamomile tea, but I felt calmer than I had since Dalton first appeared in my kitchen.

"Have you seen her spirit?"

His brows drew together. "No."

"Then she must still be alive. I don't really understand how the afterlife works, but there's one thing I'm sure about. If Violet were on the other side, she would have found you."

The answer pleased him. "I want to be with her more than anything, but not like that. I want her to live her life to the fullest and I'll be waiting for her when she finally passes away from old age."

"You really love her, don't you?" I knew the answer, but I saw how happy it made him to talk about her.

"I do." His voice was full of warmth and affection. "She helped me turn my life around. We had so many plans. We wanted three kids—two girls and a boy. Violet had a house picked out..."

I let him talk, asking the occasional question. I

couldn't explain to someone who hadn't had the experience, but I found a certain peace to having a friend who's a ghost. With no need to be anywhere else, they seemed to make time slow down.

When the evening grew cooler, I went inside and returned with a blanket. I don't think Dalton even noticed I'd walked away.

The sound of his voice against the backdrop of the waves settled my nerves and I even dozed off for a moment. Slowly the ghost's glow faded until he disappeared completely, leaving me to gaze out at the moonlit ocean alone.

CHAPTER 14

The late-night talk drained Dalton's batteries, but restored mine. I woke up the next day armed with a plan, one that I hoped would help us find Violet and catch a murderer.

Before I went down to share my idea with Jennifer, however, I called Freddie. "Hey, do you know the health inspector?"

"I do," she said, "and I was just about to call you. He ate at TacoTaco last night and came down with a case of food poisoning. From what I hear my bursting piñata description pretty much describes his current condition to a T."

"Ewww," I said, wrinkling my nose. "TMI, Freddie."

She laughed. "Sorry. But the good news—for you at least—is that you have at least twenty-four hours before he shows up on your doorstep."

"Perfect. Can you come over after work?"

"Sure. What do you need me to do?"

"Act as a stand-in inspector. We're going to clean

every nook and cranny in this place until it sparkles, and we'll keep at it until you give us a passing grade."

"I'm in. See you later."

As we signed off, I went downstairs to find Jennifer preparing to make French toast.

"Look at you!" I said, eyeing the sliced bread and a shallow bowl containing an egg and milk mixture for dipping. "When did you learn to cook?"

"I haven't really," she said, turning the heat up under a non-stick skillet, "but I'm trying. For some reason, now that Chef is gone, I wanted to try some of his recipes. I wanted to surprise you."

"You didn't have to do that, but I never say no when someone's willing to cook for me. How did shopping for Whisk go?"

"We had a blast! Zoe bought him a canopy bed, but not a floofy one since he's a boy cat. Irma insisted on getting him a bunch of catnip toys. She says everyone needs a little whacky weed every now and then. You should have seen the way he was drooling and rolling around on the floor."

In our acquaintance, Whisk had always been sedate and dignified. It sounded like his life with Zoe would be far more exciting and indulged.

Showing a commendable talent for multi-tasking, Jennifer set a plate of French toast with maple syrup and a steaming cup of coffee in front of me at the same time.

I took a bite and closed my eyes with pleasure. "This is really good."

Blushing, she said, "I want to be able to help more

around here, especially if you change your mind about letting Irma serve dinner. You are going to change your mind, aren't you?"

A gust of wind disturbed the air. "Uh oh," Jennifer said. "Is that ghostly company we know, or someone new?"

I half expected it to be our resident ghost Norma, since she only communicated by disturbing the air currents. Although I'd never seen her spirit, she made her presence known whenever anyone spoke less than kindly about her.

This spirit I could see. "Dalton just walked in. He's standing right beside you."

Jennifer turned her head and spoke to what was, for her, thin air. "Good morning, Dalton. I'm sorry you can't eat, or I'd fix you some French toast too."

Pausing long enough to say thanks—which I conveyed on his behalf—the ghost said in an excited voice, "I've remembered something, and I think it might be important."

"He says he's remembered something," I told Jennifer. "What is it?"

"The night we opened the play, a single red rose was delivered to Violet's dressing room. She thought I sent it, but I didn't. It said, 'After tonight, we can be together.'"

My mouth dropped open. "And you're just now telling me this? Why didn't Violet tell me about it?"

Dalton gave me a guilty look. "I told her it was from me so she wouldn't worry. Actors get creepy notes all the time—it's not a big deal. Or at least not usually. But this one must be from the murderer, don't you see? Someone killed me so they could be with Violet." He kicked at one of the cabinets, and Jennifer jumped at the sound. "What's wrong with me? Why didn't I remember the note sooner?"

"You died not long afterward," I said softly, hoping to soothe his self-anger. "And since you didn't think much of it at the time, it's not surprising you didn't remember."

The note on opening night shifted blame away from Violet and onto... who? My mind returned to the previous day when I met Brandon and Violet. I pictured him with his arm possessively around her waist. Kelly had admitted that several men were ready to swoop in as soon as Violet recovered from her grief. How many suspects were there?

Jennifer cleared her throat and prompted me. "I know you like having secrets with your new ghost boyfriend, but what did he say?"

I almost laughed at her comment, but this was no time for levity. "Violet got a note on opening night— the night Dalton died."

When I told her what the note had said, she became insistent. "You have to go back to Stockville. If someone killed Dalton to be with Violet, what if Violet doesn't want to be with them? They could turn violent."

Dalton became agitated. "Is she right?"

I answered both of them at once. "I hope not. And here I thought Kelly was the most likely suspect."

Jennifer raised an eyebrow. "There's nothing saying it can't be Kelly who's obsessed with Violet."

If Violet started putting the pieces together herself and figured out who had killed Dalton, what might that someone do to protect themself?

I groaned when I remembered the upcoming inspection. "I still have my business to worry about. The health inspector's stomach troubles only bought me a one-day reprieve. That doesn't exactly give me time to go gallivanting off to Stockville."

Jennifer went into instant problem-solve mode. "You go back to Stockville with Dalton, and I'll call Irma and Zoe. You're in this mess because of us. We'll clean this place within an inch of our lives. I promise that awful inspector won't find one thing to complain about."

Dalton chimed in with his own pleading appeal. "Please take her up on the offer. After all this, you can't possibly be willing to let anything happen to Violet."

He was right. The whole chain of events was starting to look like a series of accidents that needed to stop before someone else died.

"Okay," I said, reaching for my car keys. "Jennifer, I'm leaving you in charge."

"I won't let you down," she said with such earnestness, I pulled her into a spontaneous hug.

"You never have, and I'm not worried you'll start now. I'll let you know when I'm on my way back."

This time on the long drive, I almost felt like the ghost sitting next to me in the passenger seat was a living, breathing person. Dalton seemed infused with a new animating purpose—and his thinking had grown sharper along with his energy level.

"We need to go straight to Brandon's when we get back to Stockville," he told me. "He must know where Kelly lives."

"Dalton..." I kept my eyes on the road driving as fast as I dared on the winding coast highway. "Have you ever thought that Brandon might be in love with Violet?"

He shook his head vigorously. "He's my best friend."

"I'm not saying he would have acted on it," *necessarily*, I added to myself. "But he seems very possessive of her. Almost, I don't know... obsessive?"

"Brandon is comforting her, that's all. And protecting her. He's doing it for me and being a good friend to her."

"You don't think he's interested in being, maybe, more than friends?"

"What are you saying?" When I didn't reply, he went on. "Brandon told me plenty of times he didn't have time to date."

That's just what I would have told someone if I was in love with their girlfriend, but I wasn't about to tell Dalton that.

"Brandon has ambitions that go way beyond community theater in Stockville. He planned to turn over the theater management to me and Violet."

"Why didn't you tell me any of this before?"

The ghost frowned, appearing to concentrate on finding the right words. "When I first woke up on this side, all I could think about was figuring out how I got this way. Then I started to realize that everything and everyone I care about still exists, even if I don't. Being dead doesn't mean you stop caring about the people you love."

Dalton's un-selfish insight took me back to my less noble moment in the kitchen the day all this started. I'd been feeling sorry for myself because I missed Chef, not focusing on his newfound happiness with Marie. Dead or alive, we should all want good things for our loved ones.

When Dalton had first appeared in the kitchen, I tried to get rid of him as fast as possible because I didn't want another ghostly companion and I certainly didn't want to get drawn into another murder investigation.

I'd let myself believe that Chef would always be there for me, helping me cook, complaining, and making me laugh. Despite all my talk to the contrary, I had never wanted Chef to leave.

Over the past few days, Dalton had showed me that friendship isn't based on the plane of existence we inhabit, or even the ability to be seen and heard. It's about wanting the best thing for the other person no matter what. Dalton might have wanted to know what happened to him, but his focus had never wavered from Violet.

One way or another, I'd make certain he got the answers he wanted on this trip to Stockville and then he'd have closure, whatever that meant for his future.

When we turned off the highway at the exit for Stockville, I followed Dalton's directions to Brandon's modest bungalow. He answered on the second knock, staring at me rudely through the crack of the door. "Aren't you gone yet?"

"I came back because I'm concerned about Violet. I haven't been able to get ahold of her."

He made a dismissive sound. "There's nothing wrong with Violet that a good therapist couldn't fix."

I frowned at his rude comment. "Can I come in?"

He opened the door wider, stepping to one side so I could enter into the tiny foyer. To the left, I spotted a long dining room table covered with copies of the play script along with mock-ups of the sets and miniature lights, some glowing.

Brandon followed my line of sight. "You interrupted me," he said crossly. "I'm fine tuning the production ahead of this weekend. Can we get this over with so I can get back to work?"

If impressing the bigshot producer required charm or even good manners, Brandon was sunk already.

"Isn't the fact that your leading lady is nowhere to be found more important than lighting design?" I asked, a little more heatedly than I intended.

My aggressive tone bothered Dalton. "There's no need to treat my friend like that."

"Look, lady," the director said. "I carried Violet around on a silver platter after Dalton died because I needed her to hold it together." He plopped into a chair, looking defeated. "Besides, I don't need Violet. What I need is Dalton."

"What do you mean?"

He took a deep breath, letting it out slowly. "I'd just

graduated from film school when 9/11 happened. I had huge plans, but no one would hire me because of how I look."

"What do you mean?" I asked. "Because you look Arab?"

He met my eyes. "I've never even been to the Middle East. But that didn't matter. I stayed in Hollywood, hoping to for some kind of break, but it didn't happen. When I met Dalton, I'd hit rock bottom. I'd stopped caring."

I glanced over at the ghost. With shining eyes, he nodded to let me know Brandon's story was true.

"He made me care again," Brandon continued. "He wanted to restore the old theater and talked me into starting our own company. I don't know how I can go on without him. This was his dream."

"Sounds like it became your dream too," I said. "Dalton wouldn't want you to give up on it, that much I know for sure."

He looked up hopefully. "You think so?"

"If Dalton were here, he would say…" I gave Dalton a questioning look, hoping he'd get my hint. He did.

"If you want to keep my memory alive," he said, and I repeated in a low voice, mimicking Dalton's, "then keep following your dreams. If you want my life and death to mean something, then let my memory be a guiding light and live your life full of passion and purpose."

Tears rolled down Brandon's cheeks. "Thank you. I can almost hear him saying just that."

As glad as I was to bring Brandon closure, I still needed to find Violet.

After sitting silently for at least a minute, I said, "Violet received a threatening note on opening night, and another one later. Did you know that?"

He nodded "Every pretty actress gets notes from admirers. Some of them are creepy, but that just goes along with the territory. You should see what people say to me on social media. Disgusting."

"I thought we were talking about Violet."

"I'm not worried about her." He let out a huff, and the arrogant Brandon returned. "She's always been flaky. That's why I asked Kelly to be her understudy. Now that's a woman with nerves of steel." Stepping past me, he walked to the front door, making it clear my visit was over. Perhaps he felt embarrassed by what he'd shared with me or for crying in front of a woman he hardly knew.

"Don't you care who murdered your friend?" I asked.

"Please," he scoffed. "Dalton wasn't murdered."

Dalton's face turned red, and he stood with his fists clenched. "I *was* murdered!" A burst of wind jerked the screen open, then abruptly switched directions, swirling into the dining room where it scattered Brandon's papers, toppled the lights, and destroyed the miniature set.

Cursing, Brandon scrambled to repair the damage. He didn't even notice when Dalton and I left. As we went down the walk, I said, "Nice one."

The ghost gave me a questioning look. "Did I do that?"

"You sure did." I hoped he wouldn't completely lose control of his emotions. He could cause some damage, and I didn't want to be in the vicinity if that happened.

He stopped next to my car. "Now what do we do?"

"Now," I said with deliberate finality, "we go find Kelly and convince her to tell us where Violet is hiding."

CHAPTER 15

*B*y the time Dalton and I pulled up in front of Coffee Roasters, the shop was closed—in the middle of the afternoon. While we sat in the car staring at the darkened windows, half a dozen people tried the door, only to frown and walk away.

"I don't like this," Dalton said. "Kelly never closes before five o'clock. Even when we had an early rehearsal, she'd show up late to the theater rather than close early."

Privately, I worried that by showing up at her shop yesterday, I'd spooked Kelly into doing something reckless.

"Go back to the theater," Dalton suggested. "Sterling will be there. Maybe he knows something. Turn up the pressure, and you can make him tell you what he knows."

Twisting the key in the ignition, I said, "You're making me sound like the bad cop in this scenario."

The ghost grinned. "I can do it if you'd rather."

"Down, boy." I laughed. "You had your fun at Brandon's. Besides, you need to refine your ability to control the physical world before someone gets hurt. Let me handle Sterling my way." Not that I had a plan, but I'd think of something.

Dalton sulked. "Okay, but just say the word and I'll go all *Poltergeist* on him."

In less than a week hanging around with me, Dalton had gone from bumbling, reluctant specter to ghost enforcer. I considered adding afterlife coaching to my resume.

This time when I tried the theater's front door, it opened. Dalton turned up his ghostly glow to illuminate my way through the lobby and on into the auditorium, which I thought was a neat trick.

The silence of the theater unnerved me as I walked down the center aisle toward the stage where George and Pearl were cuddling on the sofa. I tiptoed past, hoping they wouldn't notice me. They'd gotten used to living people around who ignored them, and they didn't even look up.

Making my way to the backstage area, I passed by the dressing rooms on the way to the stage manger's office.

Sterling looked up from his desk and frowned when I tapped on the doorframe. "What is it? I'm really busy."

If that's how he wanted the conversation to go, I saw no reason not to be just as blunt. "I'm looking for Violet and I suspect she's staying with Kelly. I'd like her address."

Sterling's eyes narrowed. "If you want to know where Kelly lives, ask her yourself."

"I would," I shot back, "but her coffee house is locked up hard and tight. I want to talk to Kelly and make sure Violet is safe."

"Why wouldn't she be safe?"

"You tell me."

Sterling said nothing for what seemed like an entire minute. "I'm not talking to you about anything. You're trespassing. Leave now or I'll call the police."

Dalton interlaced his fingers and cracked his knuckles as if preparing to get down to work, but I shook my head, then disguised the move by saying to Sterling, "I'm leaving, but I'm going to find out where Kelly lives, because I've figured out that's where Violet is staying." I hadn't figured out any such thing, but I wanted to talk to Kelly, and I hoped Sterling would take the bait.

With that, I turned on my heel and walked out with Dalton in tow. I headed back through the darkened theater to the front door.

"Hey, lady," George called out. "Where ya goin'? I thought you was gonna find out who shot me."

I stepped up my pace, not wanting the theater ghosts to delay me. Dalton, who had been walking beside me throughout the day, was forced to float to keep up with me.

"Not that I don't like the way you deliver a line," Dalton said, "but don't you think you jumped all over Sterling a little too fast? No wonder he clammed up."

Pushing open the double doors, I broke into the

KAREN SUE WALKER

afternoon sunlight and started down the steps. "That was the plan. Come on. I need to get my car out of sight. What does Sterling drive?"

"A beat-up old Ford truck. Why?"

"Where does he park?"

"Behind the building."

"Is there another way to get out of the lot or does he have to come up the alley?"

By this time, we were both in the car and I had the key in the ignition.

"He has to use the alley," Dalton said, settling into the passenger seat. "You think he's going to go straight to Kelly's and we're going to follow him, aren't we?"

"That's exactly what we're going to do," I replied, starting the car and backing onto the street.

A voice from the back seat startled me. "Where we goin'?"

I swung around to see George. "Don't do that. You nearly made me jump out of my skin."

He lounged casually in the back seat, one elbow on the arm rest "Ah, come on, doll. You know I can't resist a good entrance. So, where to?"

Dalton answered him. "We're on a stakeout."

"A stakeout, huh? Nifty! Pearl is gonna be sore about missing out."

I drove away from the building and positioned the car behind a dumpster half a block down. From that vantage point, I had a clear view of the theater.

After a few minutes, George leaned forward. "Anyone ever say you sure know how to show a fella a good time? 'Cause if they did, they was lyin'."

160

Keeping my eyes forward, I said, "Just be glad I'm not dragging you to an exorcism."

His eyes widened and his face turned even paler than before. The ghost shimmered like a faint mirage, as if caught in a dance between worlds before he disappeared completely.

"That wasn't very nice," Dalton said, but a smile played on his lips.

"Shh." I pointed at the dark blue truck pulling out of the alley with Sterling behind the wheel. He scanned the front of the building to make sure I'd really left before turning onto the street and heading in the opposite direction.

Starting the engine, I fell in behind him, keeping a good distance between us as we passed through downtown Stockville. For a minute, I thought Sterling was headed for the highway, but then he made a left turn.

The old truck threaded through a series of neighborhoods before coming to a stop in front of a pale-yellow house with a wrap-around porch. I kept going, easing to the curb two houses down. Dalton and I both looked over our shoulders and watched as Sterling got out and all but ran up the steps.

When he pounded on the door, Kelly answered, stepping outside rather than letting the stage manager inside.

"She doesn't look happy to see him," Dalton said.

"He doesn't look happy either. I think they're arguing about something."

As we watched, Sterling tried to push past Kelly.

She stood her ground, shoving him off the porch and onto the second step.

"That does it," Dalton said. "I'm not just going to sit here. I'm going inside and find Violet."

He winked out before I could say "be careful"—which in retrospect seemed silly since bodily harm was no longer an issue for him.

Whatever Kelly said to Sterling worked. He charged down the sidewalk, jumped into the truck, peeled away from the curb, cut a sharp U-turn, and gunned the engine straight in my direction. I barely had time to dive flat in the front seat to avoid being seen.

When the truck disappeared around the next corner, I got out, walked to Kelly's front door, and knocked. Kelly opened it with a jerk, I assume expecting to find that Sterling had returned. Shock registered on her face when she recognized me.

"April. What are you doing here? How did you find out where I live?"

"Never mind about that. I know Violet is here and I want to speak with her."

Anger flashed in Kelly's eyes. "How dare you show up at my home and make demands."

Behind her, the air shimmered as Dalton materialized. "Violet is in the back bedroom. She's okay, but kinda upset."

Kelly turned to follow my gaze. "What are you looking at?"

Normally, I don't go around telling near strangers that I can see ghosts, but I couldn't think of any other way to get in that house. "I'm looking at Dalton's spirit," I said calmly. "He's standing right behind you. He says Violet is in one of the bedrooms and she seems upset."

Kelly's eyes went wide before she let out a derisive snort of laughter. "Have you lost your mind?"

"There's a blue-flowered bedspread," Dalton said, "and a figurine of a ballerina on the dresser."

"You don't seem like the kind of woman to keep a ballerina figurine. Did you take dance lessons as a child?" When I didn't get much of a reaction, I kept talking. "Violet likes the bedspread, by the way. The blue flowers are pretty."

Okay, fine. I embellished enough to sound like a psychic, but I'd spent three days hanging around a bunch of actors. The drama must have rubbed off on me.

Kelly's mouth scrunched into a frown. "What have you been doing? Lurking in the bushes and staring through the windows?"

"I'm not leaving until I talk to Violet."

"Oh, for heaven's sake," she said, glancing over her shoulder. "I don't know what game…"

Seizing the moment, I sidled into the foyer. "We just want to talk to Violet and make sure she's okay. As soon as we have, we'll leave."

"We?"

"Me and Dalton."

Her mouth opened and closed like a fish. "You and Dalton. You expect me to believe that?"

"See, the thing is, I'm not Dalton's aunt," I confessed. "I never met Dalton or had even heard of him until his ghost appeared in my kitchen asking me to solve his murder."

"His death was due to natural causes." Kelly ignored the part about me seeing his ghost.

"He overdosed on caffeine—way more than he could have gotten from drinking energy drinks. Someone added it to one of his drinks, probably the champagne you drank on opening night."

"And Dalton's ghost told you that?" she said mockingly.

I glanced over at Dalton who watched intently. "No, my local coroner did. Dalton told me that you and he didn't get along."

She smirked. "Everyone knows that."

Dalton spoke up. "She moved to this house because she wanted to start a garden. She'd always lived in apartments in L.A. and always dreamed of growing her own vegetables and planting roses."

I repeated what he told me word for word and watched her eyes widened. Dalton gave me a few more details that I couldn't possibly have known, and I shared the information with her.

"I think I need to sit down." As she stumbled toward the couch, I closed and locked the front door in case Sterling returned. When I joined Kelly, we sat at opposite ends of the overstuffed piece of furniture until she blurted out, "Ghosts aren't real."

"I didn't believe in them either," I said, "until I moved into a house that came with the spirit of a French chef in the kitchen."

"That's not possible."

"That's exactly what I thought, too. I even saw a neurologist, but it turns out there's nothing wrong with me."

She glanced nervously around the room. "You seriously want me to believe that Dalton's ghost is in this room?"

"He's standing by that bookcase."

Squinting, Kelly said, "I don't see anything." Then, squaring her shoulders, she added, "And it wouldn't matter if I did, because Violet isn't here."

"We both know that's not true. But..."

As Dalton became more frustrated with Kelly, the bookshelf began to vibrate and shake.

"Calm down, Dalton," I said in a soothing voice, hoping he'd maintain control over his new powers.

Apparently, he didn't like being told what to do because his face contorted, and a few books fell over.

"Is he doing that?" Kelly held her hands up in front of her face as if to fend off an incoming attack. "Stop it. Tell him to stop."

Stephen King's *The Shining* rocked back and forth on the edge of the top shelf.

"Fine," Kelly gulped. "You can see Violet, but you'll *both* leave after that?"

"As long as she's okay and she wants us to leave."

She stood on shaky legs. "Don't tell Violet about Dalton's ghost being here. She's been through enough already."

"I won't say a word." I crossed my fingers behind my back. After all, it wasn't my secret to keep.

elly disappeared into the back of the house and returned with Violet, who let out a cry and rushed to give me a hug. Dressed in leggings and a loose top covered in bunny rabbits, the girl looked like she might have just awakened from a bad dream at a slumber party.

"Oh, Aunt April! Thank heavens you're here! I'm so confused, I don't know which way is up. I don't know what I would have done if weren't for Kelly, but I can't stay here forever. What should I do?"

Over the top of her head, I saw a heartwarming mixture of love and relief wash away the worry that had filled Dalton's eyes for the past few hours. "She'll be okay now that she's with you," he said. "You'll take care of her."

I guided Violet to the sofa. "Let's all sit down, and you can tell me everything."

Even though I knew the story already from Dalton's eyewitness version, I thought talking might help Violet regain some of her composure. She sank onto the cushion next to me and launched into a slightly hysterical description of discovering the threatening note, and how Kelly had suggested she get away for a while.

"But I didn't want to leave Somerville, so she said I could stay with her."

Then the girl fixed me with her lovely, luminous gaze and sought confirmation that she'd done the right thing.

I wasn't sure what to say, but I tried to be encouraging. "As long as you feel safe, that's what's important."

"After what happened to Dalton, I was afraid to be in the theater." Violet's voice cracked. "I know it's terribly irresponsible of me, but with a wonderful understudy like Kelly, it's not as if the show has to shut down just because I'm not there. Right?"

At those words, the "wonderful understudy," who'd moved to a wingback chair across from the sofa, did a masterful job of appearing both concerned and humble. I was about to give that performance the great granddaddy of all bad reviews.

"Of course, you shouldn't have stayed at the theater if you didn't feel safe," I reassured Violet. "I have a different theory about the notes you received—the one on opening night and the one after Dalton's death."

Surprise registered on Violet's face. "How do you know I got a note on opening night?"

"Never mind about that right now." I could hardly explain the ghost of her fiancé had told me about it. "This may be hard for you to hear, Violet, but I believe

Kelly sent those notes to you. It's time for her to own up to her actions and explain herself."

A deep crease formed between Violet's eyebrows. "But why would Kelly do that? I don't understand." She turned toward her friend. "Kelly? What is April talking about?"

At first, I didn't think Kelly was going to answer, but then Dalton gave her some otherworldly encouragement. He leaned over and blew into her ear, then whispered, *"Tell the truth."* I doubted she could hear him, but maybe he'd somehow planted the thought in her mind.

Kelly's eyes grew wide, and she clawed at the side of her head, like she was trying to kill an enormous invisible spider.

"Kelly?" Violet gasped. "What's wrong with you?"

"Maybe her conscience is bothering her," I suggested. "Could that be the problem, Kelly?"

I'm pretty sure that even with Dalton's ghostly encouragement, Kelly still intended to double down and lie through her teeth. Dalton must have thought so, too, because this time he blew a puff of frigid breath against her cheek. From where I was sitting, it looked like the ghost used a dry ice machine to produce the effect.

Yelping, Kelly jumped to her feet and cried out, "Okay, *okay*. Fine. Just stop doing *that!* I sent the note. Just one note, though. I'm not the one who sent the rose on opening night."

Violet looked utterly crestfallen and completely

bewildered. "Why would you send me a threatening note? You're my best friend."

Kelly unleashed a torrent of pent-up frustration and jealousy. "Why? Because I wanted *my* chance. *My* chance. Do you know how it makes me feel when you just walk on stage and have everyone gushing about how wonderful you are? I work twice as hard as you do, and I never get that kind of praise, much less the big parts. Not once. When Brandon told us about the producer coming to see the play, I knew I had to figure out a way to get you to miss the performance so I could go on."

Violet's lower lip trembled. "But we're friends. Best friends."

Kelly scoffed. "Oh, really? When I had to take a part time job at the local coffee shop where you and your friends hung out, you acted like you didn't know me. That would have been bad enough, but then you made fun of me to show off to your friends. You called me Smelly Kelly. Do you remember that? Because I sure do. Sometimes when I lay in bed at night, I can hear you and the others whispering, 'Smelly Kelly' and snickering with each other."

Violet's cheeks burned bright red, and her face contorted in regret. Her voice barely more than a whisper, she said, "I can't believe I did that. I was such a terrible person."

Kelly's anger seemed to lessen at Violet's obvious distress. "I didn't mean..." She fell back in her seat. "You weren't a terrible person."

"I was," Violet insisted. "I wanted more than

anything to be popular and I did anything and every-thing I could to fit in. It wasn't worth it. Not one bit."

Having shared her long-suppressed memory, Kelly's shoulders slumped. She stared at her hands and seemed miles away.

Violet spoke softly, her voice full of regret. "Why didn't you just ask me not to play the part the night the producer's coming to see the play?" she asked without a trace of ire or ill will. "If I had known how much it meant to you, I would have faked a cold or something."

Stunned, Kelly leaned forward in her chair. "You would have?"

"Of course. You're my friend, and I love you. I had no idea how you felt. If you'd only told me, we could have found a way to fix it."

"See?" Dalton said, looking at me. "I told you she was an angel brought down to earth."

Witnessing Violet's guileless generosity, I had to agree with him, but Kelly wasn't off the hook yet—something even Violet realized.

"I understand why you wanted to scare me," she said, "but why on earth did you have to get Sterling involved? He was just an innocent bystander."

Kelly tilted her head to one side. "What are you talking about?"

"Giving him the note," Violet said. "And pushing him off the stage. He could have been really hurt."

"I didn't do anything to Sterling," Kelly insisted.

I'd begun to doubt Kelly had murdered Dalton, especially after learning that she hadn't given Violet the single rose and note on opening night. But I figured I might as well ask her. "Did you kill Dalton?"

The question had the effect of an electric shock on Kelly and Violet.

"*No!* I did *not* kill Dalton," she said emphatically. "He wasn't my favorite person, but Violet loved him, so I tried my best to get along with the guy. I didn't murder him, and I *didn't* send that note to Sterling. I never wanted to hurt anyone, I just wanted to keep Violet offstage Saturday night. I know it was selfish of me."

She spoke with so much conviction, my gut told me Kelly was finally telling the truth, but that put us back at square one. "If you didn't send the note to Sterling, who did? Brandon?"

"Oh, come on," Kelly said. "The first time you saw Sterling talking to Violet, you thought he had a crush on her. Maybe you were right. Maybe he sent the note to himself to get her attention."

I couldn't argue with her logic, but more had happened to the stage manager than that. "I could buy that story if Sterling's involvement stopped with the note, but someone pushed him off the stage." No sooner were the words out of my mouth than the all-too obvious truth slammed me in the face. "Unless he faked that too," I mumbled.

As the pieces of the puzzle fell into place, I couldn't shake off the realization that Sterling had a motive to kill Dalton. He was in love with Violet. The note he'd received and his fall had been faked to throw suspicion away from him.

"Do either of you remember what Sterling was

doing after your opening night performance when you were getting ready for your champagne toast?"

"Of course," Kelly said. "He was the one pouring the champagne. He spilled a little and ran backstage for a towel."

"I remember now." Violet's gaze went from Kelly to me as the truth dawned on her. "He topped off the last glass and handed it to Dalton."

"That's right!" Dalton rubbed his brow as the memory returned. "Why couldn't I remember that sooner?"

"Sterling put the caffeine in the glass." Everything made sense now. "He killed Dalton."

The sound of slow, over-exaggerated clapping came from the hallway. "Very good," Sterling said. "It took you long enough to figure that out, *Aunt* April."

Kelly jumped up from her chair. "How did you get in here? I told you not to come back."

The stage manager answered with an arrogant smirk. "You know, Miss High and Mighty, you really should keep your back door locked, especially if you're sheltering someone from a dangerous murderer."

Dalton's eyes widened and he balled his hands into tight fists. The ground began to tremble.

"Earthquake!" Violet, wide-eyed, ran to the doorway and held onto the door jamb. The rumbling quickly subsided, and she sighed in relief.

"It's just a minor aftershock," Sterling said. "Get your things, Violet, and let's get out of here."

"What?" Violet looked from Sterling to me, her eyes questioning. "Where are we going?"

"You're not going anywhere with him." I rushed to her side and put a protective arm around her. I didn't know how to get us out of this mess, but I hoped Dalton would help if needed.

"You killed my fiancé?" Violet clutched my arm as if she were about to crumple onto the floor. "How could you do something so evil? Why?"

"We belong together, baby," Sterling cooed. "You and me. Dalton was in the way, don't you see?"

He reached out for her hand, but she recoiled. "You disgust me."

With a simpering smile, he took a step closer to her. "As long as Dalton was around, you couldn't see that fate meant for us to be together. I know you can't see it now, but you will just as soon as I get this mess cleaned up."

Her eyes went wide. "What do you mean cleaned up?"

Sterling shook his head as if he really regretted the next words out of his mouth. "I hadn't planned to hurt anyone, but I couldn't figure out any other way to get what I wanted. Slipping the caffeine into Dalton's champagne was easy. Everyone knew how he guzzled down those energy drinks. No one would have questioned his death if *Aunt* April here hadn't shown up in town. But don't worry, honey. I'll get rid of her and Kelly and then you and I can start our lives together."

"With a million dollars to help?" My intuition told me he wasn't in love with Violet. It was the money she'd soon get that he was after.

"You're a little too smart for your own good." Sterling smirked. "Not that it's going to help you now."

Dalton's eyes widened. "Now I remember what connected him to the plot of the play. I once made a joke about him having a sterling reputation, and he didn't get it. If his name was really Sterling, he would have heard jokes like that his whole life."

"What's your real name, Sterling?" I asked.

His eyes narrowed. "Who told you?"

"Dalton figured it out before he died," I fibbed. "He left me a message that I didn't understand at the time about a connection between the play and you. In the play, the main character lied and said his name was Earnest. Were you lying to cover up your background? Or to create a new one?"

"I'd stopped in at Kelly's coffee place and overheard Dalton bragging to her about how he'd just bought a million-dollar insurance policy with Violet as his beneficiary. I'd been looking for a new opportunity. All I had to do was make a fake resume with a few buddies to answer the phone if they called to check references. Dalton and Brandon hired me on the spot."

Dalton's mouth hung open, stunned by what he heard. The shock must have drained his energy because he became more transparent to my eyes.

I glanced at Kelly, and we locked eyes. Violet might not be much help, but Kelly and I might be able to overpower Sterling especially if we caught him off guard. I nodded, letting her know I was ready when the chance came.

Tears filled Violet's eyes, but she straightened and

said in a clear, strong voice. "I'll never go anywhere with you."

Sterling spoke in a soothing voice. "You'll see. Everything's going to be great."

"No," Violet said firmly. "Nothing will ever be great again because you killed the only man I ever loved."

Sterling grabbed Violet by both arms and put his face inches from hers. "You're going with me whether you like it or not. I'll let you go as soon as the insurance money is in my hands."

As the ground rumbled again, thanks to Dalton, she used all her strength to pull away. "You're a monster, and I hate you."

Almost as if he'd thrown an internal switch, Sterling's eyes went flat. "It would have been easier my way, but I'll make it work. If you go along with my plan willingly, I might let you live. I've already killed once, remember?"

CHAPTER 17

Sterling's threat shocked us all into silence. Dalton slipped through the floor up to his knees.

"Be strong," I whispered to him.

Sterling hissed at me. "You shut up." He pulled out a gun from inside his jacket, dashing any hopes I had that the three of us could overpower him. Talking to himself, the stage manager surveyed the room like he was setting the stage for a play. "Now, how can I make your deaths look like a careless accident?" He paced from one end of the room to the other while we watched helplessly.

"You don't have to kill us, Sterling," Kelly said, her voice friendly. "Just tie us up and leave town. By the time—"

Sterling interrupted her. "This is an old house. Do you have gas heating, Kelly?"

Her jaw dropped. "You expect me to help you work out the details of a double homicide?"

"Well," he said reasonably, "you do have a good eye for stagecraft. I mean, we could go with a candle burning too close to the curtains, but if the cops found you all tied up, that wouldn't look right."

Dalton seemed to come out of a trance. "He's going to kill you and Kelly?"

I nodded, glad he could think of us while his true love was in danger. Dalton had been angry enough to whisper words in people's ears and create frigid drafts, but did he have enough energy left to take down a homicidal maniac?

Sterling, who had been pacing while he worked out how to kill us, stopped in front of an eight-shelf bookcase that reached almost to the ceiling.

"What do you think Dalton would have to say about you?" I asked Sterling.

Sterling laughed. "Dalton's dead. He can't say anything about me."

"Not now," I agreed, "but he said plenty in life. He thought you were incompetent. The only reason they kept you on at the theater was because he and the others felt sorry for you."

He shrugged off the insult. "You've been lying to us ever since you showed up in this town. How can you know all that if you and your *nephew* haven't spoken in years."

"Because I told her," Violet said, her voice taking on an antagonistic edge. Kelly was right, the girl did have stage presence when she needed it. "He said you were a loser, and I agree."

Dalton's pale form brightened. "That's my girl! You tell him."

Even though he planned to kill her after he stole all her money, Violet's words still wounded Sterling. "You don't mean that."

She had more to say. "You think you're so superior to Dalton and the rest of us, but people loved him. I can't imagine anyone ever loving you."

Turning to her, I said, "Sterling preys on others to compensate for his inadequacies."

Kelly chimed in. "You were the worst stage manager I ever worked with. I would have fired you if it were up to me."

She delivered the insult too well. Sterling took two steps and slapped her hard across the face. "Shut up," he snarled, wheeling toward Violet. "And you shut up, too, or you're next."

"Now he's gone too far," Dalton snapped. A faint current of energy surrounded him and everything in the room began to shake, including the bookcase.

When a crystal vase rocked off a shelf and crashed into pieces, I yelled to the others, "Get down!" and gave Sterling a hard shove.

As Sterling backed into the bookcase, Dalton put all his energy into toppling it over with Sterling underneath. It fell with a loud crash, books flying everywhere.

The murderer lay half-conscious and groaning on the floor under the bookcase. I grabbed the gun from where he'd dropped it.

Wide-eyed, Violet said, "Was that an earthquake?"

"Of a sort." I nodded at Dalton, who stood over Sterling, prepared to go into action again if the killer tried to escape. "Kelly, call the police."

While I stood pointing a gun at Sterling's limp figure, Violet sobbed. Whether it was out of relief for surviving the ordeal or grief over learning the truth about Dalton's death, I couldn't have said.

Later, as a Stockville deputy led the stage manager out of the living room in handcuffs, Sterling looked at me with as much venom as he could muster, considering both of his eyes were turning black and blue. A trickle of blood made its way down his forehead.

"I don't know how you pulled this off," he snarled, "but you're going to be sorry."

"No, she's not," Dalton whispered into his ear. "You're the one who's going to be sorry. I'll come see you in your jail cell, Sterling. We'll have a nice long talk."

All the color drained from the killer's face. "What was that?"

"Come on, buddy," the cop said. "Let's get you out of here."

Moving to the other side of the cuffed man, Dalton gave him a little shove.

"Who shoved me?" the stage manager shrieked. "Stop that!"

"No one shoved you," the policeman assured him. "But don't worry, we have a nice, safe cell with your name on it."

When the lead investigator told us we'd need to come down to the station and sign our statements, I explained that I lived out of town and had pressing business at home.

"Swing by on your way out of town and we'll have the statement typed up and ready."

"Thank you," I said. "I appreciate that more than you know."

We watched through the window as they stuffed Sterling in the back of a squad car and drove away. After the officers left and closed the door behind them, Violet dissolved into tears. Kelly sat beside her and put a tentative hand on her friend's shoulder.

"I'm so sorry, Violet. I had no idea Sterling killed Dalton. I thought he must have died from a heart attack or something after too many of those energy drinks."

"I thought so too," Violet agreed through her sobs.

"I let jealousy and envy get in the way of our friendship. Can you ever forgive me?"

Violet pulled Kelly into a hug. "You can be a real blockhead sometimes, you know that?"

When they'd both cried their hearts out, Kelly wiped her eyes and looked at me. "Thanks for everything. And thank… well, you know."

Dalton hovered nearby, listening to every word, happy that his one true love was safe and out of danger thanks to him.

"Don't you think she deserves to know?" I asked.

"There's more?" Violet groaned. "I don't think I can take any more surprises."

I waited for Kelly to give the okay, since she'd made

me promise not to tell Violet that I'd brought Dalton's ghost with me.

"Fine," she sighed. "With everything she's been through, why not one more major shocker?"

"What is it?" Violet's eyebrows grew together. "You're starting to worry me."

"This one I think you'll like," I said. "First, I'm terribly sorry, but I have been lying to you. My name is April May, and I run a tearoom in Serenity Cove. I'm not Dalton's aunt. I got involved in all of this because he asked me to come to Stockville to protect you from his killer."

Violet stared at me with red-rimmed eyes. "Dalton asked you? When?"

Steeling myself for rejection, I said, "His ghost asked me. I've seen ghosts before, and somehow, he ended up in my kitchen. He wanted me to solve his murder, but most of all, he wanted to make sure you were safe."

"Oh..." Violet blinked a few times. "Did you say his ghost?"

I took a deep breath and went for it. "He's here in the room with us."

"Here." Violet looked around the room. "Dalton is here?"

I told myself to be patient. It took me some time to get used to the idea of ghosts and I was able to see one. I was expecting her to trust me when I just told her I'd lied to her. That was asking a lot.

"You don't believe in ghosts?" I asked tentatively.

She grinned. "Dalton is here?"

"Yes!" Maybe this would be easier than I thought. "He told me you were an angel, and I have to say I agree. He's incredibly proud of you, you know."

"I'm more than proud," Dalton said, sitting on Violet's opposite side. "I love her more in this moment than I think I ever have."

Before I could tell Violet that he was beside her, she turned on the cushion and put out a probing hand. "Is he here?"

"Yes, you're touching his chest."

"Oh, Dalton," she said, her voice falling to a hoarse whisper. "I could always feel you close by. You'll stay with me, won't you?"

The ghost looked at me. "Tell her what I'm saying, okay?"

I nodded.

"Violet, I will always love you," he said tenderly. "A part of me will be with you through everything you face in life. We'll see each other again someday, I promise. I want you to do enough living for the both of us, starting with Saturday night's performance. Go live your dream. Do it for yourself. Do it for me. Do it for us, my love."

When I repeated the message, Violet buried her head in her hands. Kelly put an arm around her friend's shoulder.

Dalton looked on, his expression serious. "Tell Kelly to take care of Violet for me, and if she ever pulls a stunt like that note again, I'll be back."

I repeated his warning which had the desired effect. Kelly crossed her heart and promised to be a faithful and supportive friend from now on, but by the time she said the words, Dalton was gone.

When I stood to leave, Violet stopped me. "You can't go now. Stay and see Saturday's show. Please."

"If I only could, I would love to." I meant every word. "But I have to get back to my tearoom. I'll come back and see you in another performance, I promise."

"How can I ever thank you?"

"By wowing that producer and doing exactly what Dalton said you should do and living your dream."

When I got back in my car, I said tentatively, "Dalton?"

There was no answer. A pang went through me. I would have liked to have had my own good-bye with Dalton, but the temptation to hold him on the earthly plane as I'd wanted to do with Chef wasn't there. The last few days had been about finding peace for a troubled spirit. I drove back to Serenity Cove, satisfied that I'd done my job.

CHAPTER 18

*B*ack in Serenity Cove, the only cars parked in front of my house belonged to Jennifer, Irma, and Freddie. Even though I knew Irma wouldn't dare pull any more stunts until I was out of hot water with the city, I'd still held my breath when I came around the corner. With Irma, you could never be quite sure.

When I opened the back door, I found my exhausted friends camped out around the kitchen island eating take-out pizza. Before I could even set foot in my own house, Irma started barking orders at me.

"*Stop!* Put on a pair of booties."

"Booties?" I asked with a frown. That's when I realized that white paper crime scene booties covered their shoes. New plastic tarps protected the floor on either side of the island, and a third draped the eating surface. "What on earth is all this?"

"I brought the booties from the office," Freddie

explained. "These three have scrubbed this place from top to bottom. We made sure there's no trace that Whisk was ever here, even in the attic. You could eat off the floor up there."

That news alone was almost worth all the trouble of the last few days. I'd been putting off cleaning the attic since the day I moved in.

"When that inspector walks in here tomorrow, he won't find so much as a speck of dust," Freddie continued. "I've also reached out to a colleague to discuss code compliance. There's a form upstairs on your desk to fill out to get your license amended to serve hard liquor. You won't get fined for the other night because we have signed affidavits from everyone who was here that the gathering was a private dinner party."

Stunned, I said, "But what about the money Irma made?"

"I gave it back," she said, looking as if the words cost her a tremendous effort. "Nobody who was here liked hearing that the mayor was going after this place. You've gotten pretty doggone popular around this town, you know."

Since I'd arrived in Serenity Cove out of nowhere and impulsively decided to settle down, the idea that members of the community would come to my aid meant the world to me.

"No," I admitted, speaking around a massive knot in my throat. "I didn't know."

"Don't be mad," Jennifer said, "but I talked to Sheriff Fontana about what happened. He's Freddie's 'colleague' who got the form for you to fill out to change your license. We wanted to make sure to have the official version instead of one off the Internet in case the mayor could figure out a way to invalidate it."

Even though I'd processed the part about the form, my brain came to a halt at the mention of the sheriff's name. Blinking, I said, "Sheriff Fontana brought the form over in person?"

"Yeah," Irma said, "and he stayed to help us clean for the rest of the day. I love a man who can sling a mop around a kitchen."

Anderson Fontana mopped my kitchen floor, and I missed it?

"We used industrial strength sticky rollers all over the first floor," Zoe said. "They picked up a lot of lint, but not one cat hair. I told you Whisk knew the rules."

Laughing at her fervid defense of the cat, I said, "How is my former attic tenant?"

"He's the most wonderful boy in the whole world," she said, pulling out her phone and showing me a series of pictures and videos showing Whisk batting foam balls around Irma's living room.

"How do you feel about all this?" I asked, looking over at my crotchety friend.

She faked a diffident shrug. "Makes the kid happy. That's all that counts."

"Yeah, right," Zoe scoffed. "Check this out."

Passing the phone to me again, I gaped at an image of Irma sound asleep in an enormous recliner with Whisk sprawled on her lap.

When we all looked at her, Irma said, "What? Summer's not here yet, you know. The cat's warm." She gave me a smirk and changed the subject. "Tell us what happened in Stockville."

Snagging a piece of the pizza for myself, I launched into the story. The others asked probing questions and gasped at the right moments.

When I finally finished, Jennifer asked, "Did Dalton really leave without saying good-bye or even thanking you?"

"I think he had better places to be," I said, "or at least I *hope* he did."

"Are we going to find out how Saturday night's performance goes for Violet?" Zoe asked. "I don't even know her, and I want the producer to love her."

"I promised Violet that I'd make it back down there before the end of the run to see the production live. You're all invited."

"Road trip!" Zoe said, exchanging a high-five with Jennifer.

Carefully scraping up the crumbs on the tarp, Freddie said, "I'm not sure I would have been as forgiving as Violet. I don't think I would have spoken to Kelly again."

Irma harumphed. "I *know* I wouldn't have forgiven Kelly. But what a creep Sterling turned out to be. Although I don't think creep quite covers it. A murderous creep, maybe?"

"Well," Freddie said, "we're glad to have you home. I have an early appointment tomorrow, so I'm out of here. Good luck with the inspection. Let me know as soon as you get the results."

Hugging her, I said, "Thanks to all of you, I don't think I'll be needing any luck."

After Freddie exited through the back door, Irma slid off her stool. "We'd better get going, too."

"Oh, no you don't," I said. "Jennifer, Zoe, would you mind going upstairs so Irma and I can talk?"

A panicked look came over both girls' faces, and I chuckled. "Calm down," I told them. "Nothing bad is going to happen."

They picked their way across the tarps and left with nervous backward glances.

Once they'd gone, Irma's demeanor turned serious. "No bloodshed," she said. "We just got this place clean."

"You got it," I agreed. "I want to talk about the future of the restaurant."

Interest sparked in her eyes. "Future?"

"*If* we do this, how would it work? I want my home to stay a tearoom, and not turn into a full-fledged restaurant seven nights a week. But I thought maybe if we hosted a Mermaid Café popup on Friday and Saturdays, I could handle that."

Irma grinned. "That's fine for starters."

I scowled. "You're not listening, Irma. If we're going to do this, you're going to have to learn to listen."

Irma stared at her hands and mumbled, "You're right."

"What was that?" I asked. "I'm not sure I heard you."

"You're right. Friday and Saturday nights sounds great. Those were always my busiest nights anyway. And I'm not getting any younger, you know. Do you think…?" She hesitated, making me worry what she was about to suggest.

"Do I think what?"

"Could I help out with the tearoom sometimes? Your lunch offerings could use a little jazzing up. I've got some great ideas—if you want to hear them, that is."

"Let's start with dinner, first, okay?" I suggested, not wanting to put a damper on her enthusiasm, but not wanting her to get carried away either.

"I'd suggest closing from four to five o'clock to transition from the tearoom to dinner service," Irma said, adding, "on Fridays and Saturdays." She paused. "And maybe Sundays?"

I laughed. "You're incorrigible. Fridays and Saturdays for now. I like my quiet Sunday evenings to unwind after a busy weekend."

"And since we're a pop-up with a limited menu," Irma continued, obviously having given it a lot of thought, "I thought we'd have themed evenings—steak, seafood, Italian, and even Mexican. You get more customers when they think they're coming in for something special that they can't get regularly."

"You're not worried about competing with Taco-Taco in the Mexican food department?" I asked.

Making a scoffing sound, Irma said, "You've clearly never eaten my enchiladas."

Drumming my fingers on the island, I said, "While I was in Stockville, Kelly and I talked about the potential of my adding a coffee room in the library. That could work in the evenings too if we served brandy or after-dinner drinks. We could host special events, too."

Now fully excited, Irma said, "Now you're talking."

Still concerned, I said, "Do you think we can do this without harming our friendship?"

Looking me straight in the eye, Irma said, "Yes, because I won't lie to you again. That was a rotten thing to do. I make mistakes, but I don't repeat them."

"Fair enough," I said, putting out my hand to seal the deal with a shake. "Let me get this license business figured out and we'll start planning a proper opening—one where we get to keep the profits."

Later that night, I filled out the form to extend the terms of my liquor license. Running my fingers over the paper, I pondered Anderson Fontana not only going to the trouble to get the document for me, but pitching in to help get my tearoom ready for the health inspector.

Glancing at the clock, I saw it was only 9:30. Not too late for a text message. Using my thumbs, I typed, *Hi. Heard about you helping today. Thanks so much.*

Three dots appeared on the screen. My heartbeat shifted into high gear as I waited to read the incoming message.

My pleasure. No love lost between me and the mayor. How'd things go in Stockville?

This was the moment of truth. I could either peck out a ridiculously long text message or tell the man in person.

Coffee on my front porch at 8 tmrw? Not allowed to get kitchen dirty.

The dots appeared again followed by a laughing face emoji. Then a message. *Coffee and doughnuts on me. It's a date.*

At the sight of the word "date," my stomach gave an excited flutter.

Uncertain what to type next, I went with, *Good night.*

Good night. Sleep well, April.

Sleep? Not a chance.

After I changed into my pajamas, I got under the covers and turned out the light. The full moon shining through the window bathed my bedroom in an other-worldly glow.

When something rustled outside, I sat up and said, "Dalton? Is that you?"

There was no answer, just the brush of a branch against the siding. Sighing, I slid back under the covers, chiding myself for being so selfish. The first time I met Dalton, I fed him the standard admonition about going into the light. Now here I was trying to draw him back onto the worldly plane.

"Go to sleep, April," I admonished myself. "Dalton got the answers he needed, and you solved his murder. Take the win."

There was just one problem. In the silence of the night, it didn't feel like a win.

The wind whispered, and I could have sworn it said, "April?" I blinked and Dalton's form shimmered into view.

"You're still here." I smiled despite myself, happy to see him again. "I thought you were moving on."

"I had to say good-bye." His radiant smile warmed my heart.

The soft roar of a motor came from outside. I got out of bed and shuffled to the window, pulling back the curtains. I gasped at the sight of a small plane soaring overhead. It did a loop-de-loop then circled back.

"Your parents?" I asked, doing my best not to tear up.

He nodded. "Thank you, April. I'll never forget you."

I sniffed as he faded from view then looked out the window in time to see the ghost plane disappear into the night.

CHAPTER 19

The next morning, I stood in front of my closet, debating what to wear and telling myself I wanted to make a good impression on the inspector, but knowing I was picking an outfit for Anderson Fontana's eyes only.

The weather app on my phone promised a moderate day with highs in the 60s, so I finally settled for a deep green sweater and a mid-calf length floral skirt. At the last minute I knotted a colorful scarf around my neck.

Standing back from the mirror, I inspected my appearance, adding a few swipes of mascara and a spritz of perfume before heading downstairs.

Jennifer's eyes went wide when she saw me. "You look gorgeous. Are you trying to impress the health inspector?"

Ducking my head in a gesture that even I knew was far too adolescent for a woman my age, I said, "Sheriff

193

Fontana is bringing over breakfast since I'm not allowed to use the kitchen."

Clapping her hands, she squealed in delight. "Finally! I didn't think you'd ever make a move."

I felt my face redden. "I did not make a *move*. I just want to thank the man for helping, and he asked about how things came out in Stockville. The story's too long to tell in a text message."

Putting on a mock serious face Jennifer said, "You're not going to believe this, April, but did you know that if you put someone's number into the phone and hit 'send' you can have an actual conversation with them? Like with your voice."

"Spoken by someone who never talks on the phone." Putting my hands on my hips, I said, "What are you even doing here? Don't you have a class this morning?"

She giggled. "I do. Now here's the plan. I'm going to leave by the back door and pull the tarp out after me. You go out the front door and do the same thing."

"And do what with the tarps?"

"Shove them in the trunk of your car or something, I don't care. The point is, do *not* walk on the floors until the inspector gets here."

Snapping a salute, I said, "Yes, ma'am."

Turning serious, she said, "Don't worry about the inspection. Freddie says you'll pass with flying colors. Text me when it's over."

"I'm not worried," I fibbed. "Now go so you won't be late."

Following her instructions, I went out through the

front of the house and was folding the tarp from the tearoom floor when Sheriff Fontana came up behind me. "Need some help with that?"

He looked especially handsome in the early morning light with the sun glinting on the hints of silver in his sandy hair. Putting two cups of coffee and a bag of pastries on the table at one end of the porch, Fontana helped me reduce the unwieldy tarps to neat squares, which he shoved under one of the chairs to get them out of the way.

When we were seated across from one another, the Sheriff said, "How'd you sleep?"

"With everything going on lately, it took me a while to fall asleep. How about you?"

"Let's just say I'm looking forward to this coffee to get my blood pumping." He pried the lid off and took a sip. "Don't tell Jennifer, but that frothy stuff she makes is better."

Before I thought about it, I said, "Come by any morning and have a cup."

A slow smile spread across his face. "I'll take you up on that. Tell me about Stockville."

Fontana listened to my story from beginning to end as I gave him a ghost-less version of the events. His eyes widened when I came to the conclusion. "What do I have to do to get it across to you that confronting murderers without backup isn't a good idea?"

"Believe me, I've learned my lesson." Besides, I told myself, I'd had Dalton for backup, and he came through with flying colors.

Taking another croissant out of the bag, the Sheriff looked at me questioningly. "Want half?"

"Sure."

He broke the pastry in two and handed a piece to me. Our fingers grazed in the exchange, leaving my skin tingling at the unexpected touch.

"I have one question," he said, chewing contemplatively.

"What's that?"

"How did you get interested in Dalton Banks' murder in the first place? I hope you're not trolling newspapers looking for interesting killings. Homicide isn't a hobby."

"Well, it's… You see, I… there's this…"

What a time to forget how to speak the English language.

Fontana tilted his head and considered my incoherent babble. Then, he said something that melted my heart. "You can tell me anything, April."

The memory of how badly this same conversation had gone with Mark rose in my mind, but if there was the slightest chance of a relationship between me and the sheriff, it wasn't going to be built on excuses and half-truths. So, I decided to tell him the truth and see what happened.

"I ended up in Serenity Cove completely by chance when I got a flat tire," I began. "The first time I saw this house I fell in love with it and bought it. It was completely impulsive, but it worked out great."

"I think so," he said.

I felt my cheeks redden. "When I moved into this

house, I discovered…" I took a deep breath and finished my sentence. "There was a ghost."

"A ghost?" he repeated.

I cleared my throat. "The ghost of Chef Emile Toussaint was living in my kitchen." I held my breath and waited for laughter or derision.

The sheriff said, a smile playing on his lips, "A chef? I suppose he taught you how to cook."

"I'm serious," I insisted. "And I already knew how to cook. But he did teach me how to make a wonderful bechamel sauce. And his coq au vin is to die for."

He nodded, and I could tell he didn't know what to think.

"Say something?" I begged. "Please?"

"So, what does this have to do with Dalton Banks' murder?"

"Well… his ghost came to see me and asked me to solve his murder." Again, I waited for a laugh, but it didn't come.

To my surprise and tremendous relief, the sheriff said, "Well, that's convenient. I wish the ghosts of murder victims would talk to me. It would make my job a heck of a lot easier."

"Just send them my way," I joked. "I'll take their statement for you. I'm not sure how to get them to sign it, though."

He took a long sip of his coffee, and I suspected he was deciding how to respond to my revelation.

Finally, he shook his head. "If you tell me that you can see and talk to ghosts, I believe you. I've lived long enough to know there's a lot more to this world than most people are willing to consider possible. Me? I like possibilities."

Time seemed to stop. "You do, huh?"

"I do." Something shifted in his eyes and a slow smile spread over his handsome face. "Speaking of possibilities, my divorce papers are signed. I'm a free man and I would very much like to spend some time with you, April May—if you're interested."

Without a moment's hesitation, I said, "I'm interested, Sheriff Fontana."

He reached across the table and caught hold of my hand. "My friends call me Andy."

Like a goofball, I said, "Mine call me April."

We both cracked up at the same time, laughing until tears rolled down our cheeks. It was a good harbinger of things to come.

EPILOGUE

The first day we reopened the SereniTea Tearoom, I returned to my familiar routine, stirring pots on the stove, mixing up a batch of scones, and anticipating friends and neighbors popping in for a treat.

Jennifer had gone upstairs, and I hummed a happy tune as I patted the scone batter to the right thickness. As I pressed the cookie cutter into the dough, I heard a voice behind me and sighed.

"Hey, I thought you was gonna solve my murder?" George appeared almost solid.

With a sigh, I said, "I did." He'd been dead for nearly a hundred years, but he couldn't remember what he'd been told just the day before.

He grinned. "You did? Well, that's all right then. Who?"

I didn't look forward to telling him—again—that his girlfriend, Pearl, was the one who'd done him in. But maybe his memory wasn't the problem. Maybe the notion of Pearl as his killer was too painful a thought for his mind to hold onto. Did he keep forgetting who'd killed him so he could live a ghostly happily ever after with his sweetheart?

"It was that guy," I began, hoping he'd help fill in the gaps. "That guy who was always giving you a hard time."

George's brows knit together in concentration. "What guy? What was his name?"

"I don't remember his name," I improvised. "You two got in a big fight." When he didn't take the bait, I added, "Over a dame."

"Oh, right!" His eyes lit up. "You mean Charlie One-Ear. Yeah, I made a move on Darla. I didn't know she was his main squeeze, or I never would have tried with her. Never go after a mobster's dame."

"I'll do my best to keep that in mind." I watched over his shoulder as Pearl came into view. "Hello, Pearl."

"Hey!" George hurried over to her, excited to share his news. "Did you hear that? She solved my murder. Ain't that great?"

Pearl nodded, giving me a grateful look. "I heard."

George's face fell. "Oh, but we still don't know what happened to you." He turned back to me. "Can you solve her murder, too?"

Pearl threw an arm around his neck. "I already know what happened to me, ya big lug. I couldn't imagine my life without you, so I shot myself."

"You did?" He blinked a few times. "That's the nicest

thing anyone's ever done for me." He grabbed his ghostly partner in a passionate embrace.

"Get a room," I mumbled. When they finally released each other, I figured I'd be done with them for good now. "Now you can go back to your theater and do whatever you do when you're there."

"It's kinda boring," Pearl said. "The place is empty half the time, and besides, nobody seems to believe in ghosts anymore."

"It's getting harder and harder to scare people," George agreed.

"I've got a great idea—tell me what you think." Pearl gave me her sweetest smile. "We could help you solve murders."

"Oh, no, no, no." I wasn't a detective, so why did people act like I was? "I have a tearoom to run. I'm not in the murder solving business."

"How about the missing persons biz?" George asked. "I heard through the grapevine that there's a ghost who knows a guy who's not a ghost. He's gone missing and nobody can find him."

"I'm not in the missing person biz, either."

"Too bad." George leaned closer, lowering his voice to just above a whisper. "The ghost is watching over a shop run by two women who have some kind of special powers."

Despite my better judgment, I said, "Tell me more."

. . .

Thank you for reading *Tea is for Temptation*.
Visit Amazon to order Tea is for Taken, book 8 in the series!
Sign up for my (mostly) weekly email with updates, sales, freebies, and other fun stuff!
(Not to mention stories and pictures of my rescue dog).
https://karensuewalker.com

And read on for recipes!

RECIPES

BREAKFAST PASTRIES WITH FRUIT AND CREAM CHEESE

Yield: 8 pastries

INGREDIENTS:

- 6 ounces cream cheese at room temperature
- 2 Tablespoons sugar
- 1 teaspoon vanilla extract
- 1 17.3 ounce package—2 sheets--frozen puff pastry, thawed
- 1 ½ cups fruit – berries, peaches, plums, apples, or pears or a combination of these
- 1 large egg

INSTRUCTIONS:

1. Preheat oven to 400ºF (200ºC) and prepare two cookie sheets with parchment paper.
2. In a bowl, mix cream cheese, sugar, and vanilla until fully combined.
3. Lightly flour the surface and roll out puff pastry on top to flatten.
4. Cut each sheet of puff pastry into 9 equal squares and transfer them to the cookie sheet.
5. Lightly score a border ¼ inch from the edge.
6. Spread 1 to 2 teaspoons of the cream cheese filling in the middle inside the border, then place fruit on top.
7. Repeat with the remaining pastry squares.
8. Break egg into a small bowl and whisk with 1 Tablespoon cold water. Brush the edges of the pastries with the egg wash.
9. Bake for 15-20 minutes or until pastry is golden brown and puffed.
10. Remove from the oven and transfer to a baking rack to cool.

FUNERAL POTATOES (AKA CHEESY POTATOES)

Yield: 12 servings

INGREDIENTS:

- 28 to 32 ounce package of frozen diced or shredded potatoes (thawed)
- 16 ounces (2 cups) sour cream
- 10.5 ounce can cream of chicken soup
- 10 Tablespoons melted butter – 6 ounces for potatoes and 4 ounces for topping
- 1 teaspoon salt
- ¼ teaspoon pepper or to taste
- 1 teaspoon dried minced onion or ¼ to ½ teaspoon onion powder
- 2 cups shredded cheddar cheese (sharp or mild—jack will also work)
- 2 cups corn flakes

INSTRUCTIONS:

1. Thaw potatoes in your fridge overnight. In a pinch, you can spread them on a baking sheet and put them in a 200-degree oven for about 20 minutes.
2. Preheat oven to 350 degrees F.

3. In a large bowl, combine sour cream, cream of chicken soup, 6 Tablespoons of melted butter, salt, pepper, and dried onion or onion powder. Mix well.

4. Add potatoes and shredded cheese and combine. Transfer mixture to a 9x13" pan and spread out evenly.

5. Prepare topping by putting cornflakes in a bag and crushing them gently with your hands or a rolling pin.

6. Add the remaining 4 tablespoons of melted butter to the crushed cornflakes and mix well. Sprinkle mixture over potatoes.

7. Bake uncovered at 350 F for 40-50 minutes.

8. Serve!

OPEN FACE CUCUMBER TEA (OR APPETIZER) SANDWICHES

Yield: 20-24

INGREDIENTS:

- One English cucumber
- 4 ounces cream cheese, softened.
- 1 tablespoon mayonnaise
- 1-2 Tablespoons of minced chives (or substitute sliced green onion tops)
- 1/8 teaspoon salt, seasoned salt, or garlic powder or more to taste
- Squeeze of lemon to taste (optional)
- 8 slices white bread

INSTRUCTIONS:

- After scrubbing well, shred about half the unpeeled cucumber. Press between paper towels to remove any excess moisture.
- In a medium bowl, mix the cucumber, cream cheese, mayonnaise, minced chives or green onion tops, salt, and optional lemon juice.
- Chill the mixture—one hour or so (longer is okay).

- Prepare about 12 very thin slices of cucumber for the garnish—you'll need 24 half slices.
- When ready to assemble, cut 2-inch circles of white bread using a cookie or biscuit cutter or a drinking glass.
- Scoop about a teaspoon of the cucumber mixture onto the bread slices. Garnish with very thin slices of cucumber cut in half along with sprigs of dill if desired. Serve immediately.

April's note: The filling can be stored in the refrigerator for 2-3 days, but don't assemble the sandwiches in advance or the bread will get soggy!

BLACK FOREST CAKE IN A MUG

Yield: One Mug Cake

INGREDIENTS:

- ¼ cup flour
- 3 Tablespoons tightly packed brown sugar
- 2 tablespoons unsweetened cocoa Dutch-processed cocoa
- ⅛ teaspoon salt
- ¼ cup milk
- 2 tablespoons canola oil or other vegetable oil without a strong taste
- ¼ teaspoon vanilla extract
- 2 tablespoons chocolate chips
- 2 tablespoons cherry pie filling with about 6 cherries plus liquid
- ¼ cup whipped cream

INSTRUCTIONS:

1. Add first seven ingredients to a mug and mix well.
2. Stir in chocolate chips and cherry pie filling.
3. Microwave for 90-120 seconds until top looks dry.
4. Top with whipped cream (dusting of sifted cocoa and cherry optional)

5. Garnish with mint if desired

April's note: This isn't nearly as decadent as a Black Forest cake, but it also takes very little time to make, and there are no leftovers tempting you to overindulge!

WHAT'S NEXT FOR APRIL MAY?

TEA IS FOR TAKEN

A Haunted Tearoom Cozy Mystery #8 - Coming in late 2023

There's a new ghost in town, and he wants April to solve his murder. Is this April's new destiny—to be a ghost detective? Find out in Tea is for Temptation.

Available on Amazon

For all of Karen Sue Walker's books, visit https://karensuewalker.com/books

- *Haunted Tearoom Cozy Mysteries*
- *Bridal Shop Cozy Mysteries*
- *Arrow Investigations Humorous Action-Adventure Mysteries* by KC Walker

Milton Keynes UK
Ingram Content Group UK Ltd.
UKHW011320230823
427358UK00004B/213

9 781955 610155